T0070355

BANG! BANG!

JOHN CORRY

Also by John Corry

Philosophy

The Wisdom of Love: Philosophical Implications of 1st Corinthians 13
Paul Among the First Philosophers: a symposium on Love
The Reconciliation of Paul and Nietzsche – a postmodern symposium on love and power
Primal Words: SELF, Love, God, Jesus
Bottoms' River
Christian Theology for Porn Lovers
Theological Reflections of a Catholic Quaker (essays)
Shimmering Words – a family of essays

Religion

Something to Offend Everyone – A Christian Life
Openings, Leadings, and Dreams: listening to the inner voice of love
Forty Nine Sits
John.... Yes Lord?
Talk with Jesus, and then Go Forward.
A Short History of the Holy Spirit (2 volumes)
God's Response to Satan's Holocaust: the clash between radiant goodness and radical evil
Prelude to God's Response to Satin's Holocaust
Radiant Church: Catholic, Quaker, Bruderhof

Poetry

Heaven Our Last Beginning (a long poem)
Gospel Poems
Talimagala's Gift – Poems of Earth and Sky
Seeds of Sanctity

Travel

Three Cowboys Roam the Holy Land (with Jay Clark)
God and Art in Italy: bull sessions on the way to paradise (with Jay Clark)
The Spanish Connection (with Jay Clark)

Plays

Save the Sardines
The Resurrection of Caroline Muse
Saints (one act play in *Emails, Letters and Limericks*)
Fifty Books
Author on Stage
Jesus on Stage

Bits and Pieces

Emails, Letters and Limericks
Still Writing at Eighty Seven
Politics, Prayer, and Poetry

BANG! BANG!

iUniverse books may be ordered through booksellers or by contacting:

iUniverse
1663 Liberty Drive
Bloomington, IN 47403
www.iuniverse.com
844-349-9409

ISBN: 978-1-6632-3606-7 (sc)
ISBN: 978-1-6632-3607-4 (e)

Print information available on the last page.

iUniverse rev. date: 02/17/2022

BANG! BANG!

DISCLAIMER

Bang! Bang! is a work of fiction[1] written in late 2021 and early 2022 during the covid pandemic, which could have been over several years ago if more citizens had been vaccinated. Other problems of that era include: Climate Change, Republican efforts to restrict the voting rights of black, brown and other minority citizens, immigration, nuclear war, and possible insurrections to overthrow the election of duly elected public officials. Perhaps as never before in our history has the spirit of fear, anger, and powerlessness clouded the minds of those who'd live in the land of the free and the home of the brave.

I don't know what comes next in present time, but I would assume the conflict between the Cloud of Knowing and the Cloud of Unknowing[2], will still be with us unless God's Day of Judgement intervenes.

---

[1] Bible quotes are from the New Revised Standard Version. Characterizations of living and deceased people, places, organizations, and events are purely fictional. . Most quotes and references to people and historical events are accurate; many others are not.

[2] Of course some knowing is necessary but knowing alone, as in Goethe's Faust is self-destructive.

CONTENTS

PREFACE

A Preface is placed between the Forward, written by an esteemed authority or one of the author's close friends, and the author's Introduction which tells the reader what the book's about without giving away the ending. The Introduction is a circus barker inviting the curious to savor the odd and awesome world just behind the purple curtain. The Introduction is a professor welcoming her new class into the specifics of an area of special interest. An Introduction is foreplay which entices the reader into intimacy. An Introduction is a companion who travels with the reader on her journey to the Promised Land.

Some writers write the same book over and over; some start fresh every time, and many like me follow the same concerns in different settings book after book. Whether I'm writing poetry, religious essays, philosophy, plays, a travel book or two with Jay Clark my best friend, or a theological mystery like the two Bang books I remind myself of Prince Andrew in War and Peace lying wounded on the battlefield under the stars wondering what it's all about. Why am I – we – alive? I also remind myself of Philip Neri, the trickster saint, who in his own peculiar way knew what it's all about and wanted to share the good news with his sisters and brothers.

INTRODUCTION

As I was writing Bang! Bang! everything made perfect sense. Reading it over afterwards it seems a confusing mix of isolated incidents overflowing with forgettable characters. Well not …

WOOF!

That's the dachshund, Schatzi, who reminds me of Brunie our first….

WOOF!

…dog. She's taken the place of the Inner Voice of Love, Jesus for me, who's been interrupting my writing for over thirty years.

Woof…. ……… …. ………… ……………. arf.

Woof says get to the point, which is that Bang! Bank! is best read as a series of independent incidents and characters set within a socio-political context, which is itself set within a theological context. The good guys are working to prevent global chaos while the bad guys are promoting chaos for various religious, political, and personal reasons. As the disjointed incidents become familiar over time the plot increasingly focuses on the theological issues behind the seemingly random events.

That said the best way to read Bang! Bang! is to take your time enjoying each character, each incident, as you read. That's what I did as I was writing. I knew I was writing about the conflict between good and evil, but I put that aside to enjoy, and sometimes grieve, the characters and events as they came to me in the writing.

Since the characters come with a history based on their presence in the first Bang book I've provided a list of notable characters to help readers feel at home in Bang II.

Though author imagined media inserts (T.V., newspapers and magazines) current in the early 2020s are historically unreliable, in private conversation I would strongly defend the accuracy of my portrayal of Tucker Carlson, Henry Kissinger, and Republicans who worship, or at least pretend to worship, Donald Trump.

NOTABLE CHARACTERS

Anti Chaos

Peachbush Georgia.

Fred Corrie, father of the family. Of average interest.

Mizz Ruth Corrie. Hossie's mother.

Hossie (Jehosphat) Corrie. Chubby fifteen year old in love with Sam Cohen. Of more than average interest.

Suzie Q Corrie. Twelve year old mystic.

Rabbi Cohen. Speaks only Yiddish and Hebrew but may think in English, French, and German.

Mizz Cohen. Makes chocolate kosher pizzas for Sam and Hossie.

Sam Cohen. Hossie's sixteen year old best friend. And more.

Father Lopez. Parish priest at Our Lady of Guadalupe, across the tracks in Peachbush.

Berne Switzerland.

Hannah Hossenhoeffer. Ex-Madam President of Switzerland, loves her stout lad supporters.

Hans the smart one.

Wiggy the good-natured one.

Arnold Really O'Reilly unpublished mystery writer from Maine.

Schatzi. Arnold's lovable black and tan dachshund.

Hank Hangover popular but eccentric Haverford College professor.

Jack, ex-Proud Boy, friend of Arnold.

Pastor Sophia of St. Peter and Paul of the pope-less Reformed Catholic Church, in Berne.

Deacon Lance Lott, Sophia's husband. Dog master of 150 dogs at St. Peter and Paul.

Norbertines at Daylesford Abbey.

Abbot Joel, confidant of Pope Philip Neri.

Father Andrew, ex-pickpocket from Atlantic City on the east coast.

Sister Phyllis. The first female Norbertine in eight hundred years.

Rome.

Pope Philip Neri, born Bob Williams, choirboy from Albuquerque, New Mexico. Close friend of abbot Joel.

Pro Chaos

Haverford College

Ex-president, ex-con, Dr. Sylvester (Sly) Foxxy. Motivation? Non-religious; non-political. Out for the buck.

Coach Randalier. Coach Randy is known for his after game one-on-one shower conferences with selected players "to wash away the stain of defeat" and the "vanity of victory."

Tim Rottenburger. Graduating senior, third member of the Haverford clique, is a bright student gone bad. Tim's a nasty piece of work.

Peachbush, Georgia.

Pastor Jones organized the religious alt-right's nationwide unsuccessful plot to replace Easter with the beginning of Armageddon in the first Bang book. A powerful and persuasive preacher.

<u>Boise, Idaho.</u>

Enrique Tarrio. Cuban-American, current boss of the Proud Boys.
Jack ex-Proud Boy. Friend of Arnold Really O'Reilly.

<u>Somewhere in Texas.</u>

Senator Darlington Dewlittle. Neo-fascist Republican senator with a 50/50 chance of winning the next presidential election.

<u>Somewhere in Washington state</u>

Ron Watkins. Reputed to be "Q" behind the QAnon conspiracy which preaches that Deep State Democrats are Satanic pedophiles trafficking in worldwide sexual child abuse.

"They set out from Succoth and camped at Etham on the edge of the wilderness. The Lord went in front of them in a pillar of cloud… to lead them along the way."

Exodus: 20-21

"Alas for the day!
…For the day of the Lord is near…
a day of clouds, a time of doom for the nations."

Ezekiel 30: 2-3

PART 1

TWO CLOUDS

CHAPTER 1

SOMETHING'S AMISS

Bang!

Pause.

Bang!

Screen door? Car backfiring? Or the big one?

***

Meanwhile back in Berne ex-Swiss president Hannah Hossenhoeffer is finger drumming on her favorite equilateral triangular outdoor table at *Woof.*

Looking down fondly on Schatzi, a lovable black and tan low bellied dachshund that Arnold Really O'Reilly, an unpublished mystery writer, had shipped over from Maine, Hannah smiled. It had been a shock when the inner Voice of love, Jesus, on whom she'd depended for comfort and guidance for decades insisted her new inner guide was to be a mere badger hunting low bellied long dog, runt of the litter, but when the inner Voice insisted she had little choice. Besides she'd always liked dogs. Especially sausage hounds. Thinking of the Inner Voice brought to mind Swiss Madam ex-President Hannah Hossenhoe and her stout lads.

Arf. Woof.... ... . stout..... .... Woof?

There were four stout lads. Hans is the smart but saucy one, Wiggy the warm-hearted one, six four lean bean Arnold Really O'Reilly is an unpublished mystery writer from Maine, and Hank Hangover the only liberal Quaker theologian in North America. Ah me Hannah sighed. Alas for lads and lasses dancing on the lazy lawns of yesteryear.

WOOF!

By now Hannah had grown accustomed to the cautionary "woofs", "ruffs", and "arfs", which keep our story from wandering off into irrelevant whimsy. Occasionally the woofs and arfs came from Schatzi swishing her tail for attention, but more often the woofs come from the inner Schatzi. As the runt of the litter Schatzi had almost died on...

"Runt? You said she was the best of the litter?"

"She is."

***

Sipping her second cup of eiskaffesse, iced expresso laced with vanilla ice cream, waiting for Hans and Wiggy, Hannah banged on the table.

"Merde. Scheisse. Hans is never late... Ah at last."

"Morning Hannah. I see you're missing the hurly burly of political life."

"I'm missing you two. You're twenty minutes late."

"What you need is a challenge to rest your restless brain."

"What I need is friends who aren't too busy to be on time."

***

Bang!

"Fred?"

"Tomorrow I promise."

"Don't promise Fred. Just fix the damn screen door."

Cubby Jehosophat Corrie, now fifteen and Sam Cohen, his best friend looked up. Momma Corrie never used bad language. Something was up.

***

"I did it on my free time abbot Joel."

"Yes, Father Andrew, but it doesn't belong in Hubert's art show. It sends the wrong message."

"He put it in; not me."

"You could have stopped him. It's your… whatever you call it. A pastel pink phallic cross is not a fit entry in Daylesford abbey's annual art show. Or any other Norbertine venue."

***

"Who's Father Andrew?"

"A once lost soul with a troubled childhood who slept under the boardwalk in Atlantic City, New Jersey. Andrew was a pickpocket by day and attended the Last Chance Pentecostal Church in the evening. After seeing – not sensing – Jesus by the Steel Pier at night Andrew was guided to the Norbertines."

"Thanks."

***

"Joyful, joyful we adore you. God of glory God of love. Hearts unfold like…"

"Bueno dias. Bon jour. Good morning. Halo. You've reached the pope's answering service."

Thirty minutes later Abbot Joel at Daylesford Norbertine abbey in Paoli, Pennsylvania, had pope Philip Neri on the line for their weekly catch up call.

"……… ………... …. ………?"

"And you Holy Father?"

"Please. Just Philip. What's up?"

"I'm not sure but something's up. I checked with madam Hossenhoeffer and her stout lads. And with Father Lopez and the Corries down in south Georgia where…"

"Ruff."

"I'm quarreling with the cannons here. Hannah's growling at her friends in Berne. And the Corries are snapping at one another over a banging screen door. Something wrong. How is it in Rome?"

"Terrible. More bishops protecting their priests from prosecution for molesting altar boys – and girls. The head of Catholic relief services has been caught diverting contributions for the poor to his Swiss bank account. The American Church[3] is rife with dissention. The USCCB, the US Conference of Catholic Bishops, is threatening to defrock nuns who question their teaching on abortion or anything else. And I've got the virus. You're right Joel. Something's amiss.

If you have any thoughts on what we can do give me a call. Anytime. Pax vobiscum. Much love Joel"

"Much love Bob."

***

"Happiness is a warm gun."

"That's enough Tim. There've been enough warm guns already. The question is what can we do about it?"

"Coach Randy sir. You fail to appreciate the situation. It's over."

Pause.

Tim Rottenburger, now a senior majoring in T.V journalism smiled his friendly snarl and relaxed into the old couch in Coach Randalier's office at Haverford, a small liberal arts college in south eastern Pennsylvania.

"You were well named Tim. Rottenburger. Christ, can't you ever step back and look for solutions instead of pushing us off the cliff over every minor crisis we face? I'm tired of it. Tired of you always bitching about how fucked up the world is. Get out. I mean it. Get out of my office."

"Coach?'

"Yes?"

"Fuck you."

Tim walked to the door and left, closing the door quietly behind him.

***

Philadelphia Inquirer November 5, 2024.

TRUMP WINS

REPUBLICANS TAKE BACK SENATE

---

[3] Capitalizing Church when referring to the Catholic church reflects the way Catholics like myself colloquially refer to our particular denomination.

HOUSE WAITS ON FLORIDA RECOUNT
ALLIGATORS LEAVE EVERGLADES – Heading for Miami
FOREST FIRES RACE TOWARD SAN FRANCISO
QANON AND PROUD BOYS INVITED TO…
Ruff.

***

The congregation at the Lily White Church in the Valley, Peachbush, a small town in southern Georgia, to be distinguished from Peachtree City just south of Atlanta, is looking up to Zoom at their old reverend, Pastor Jones, behind the pulpit in *I Told You So* Pentecostal church in Tennessee. Pastor Jones looks down on his boyhood friend Deacon Bestbuddy and his old congregation.

"Pastor Jones?"

"Yes deacon."

"You see the folks behind me?"

[Waves, smiles and stamping of feet.]

"Pastor Jones. Pastor Jones. Please come home."

The chanting gradually tails off and the congregation lapses into an awkward silence.

"I'm waiting."

Pause.

Pause.

Deacon Bestbuddy slowly gets to his knees bows his head and stretches his arms out to Tennessee. The congregation follows and the wailing begins.

"We were wrong."

"Forgive us."

"We're so sorry. Please come home."

Pastor Jones smiles, but waves the congregation to remain on their knees as he preaches on God's response from *Hosea* to His faithless flock.

"How can I give you up, Ephraim? How can I turn you over O Israel? My heart recoils within me; my compassion grows warm and tender for I am God, the Holy One and I will not come in wrath. I will allure her and bring her into the wilderness and speak tenderly to her."

Hearing these heart-wrenching words the congregation weeps, moans, and beat their breasts begging for forgiveness.

Waving his old flock to their feet they settle back on the sturdy caramel colored benches to listen to the sermon they all knew is coming.

"Fallen, fallen is Babylon the great. It has become a dwelling place of demons; a haunt of every foul spirit... Come out of her my people so that you do not share in her plagues." Rev. 18.

Memories of having abandoned the good reverend with a sparsely attended farewell barbecue before setting him adrift to scrounge for a church with half the membership of Lily of the Valley still weighed on their minds. And he'd been right. Armageddon was upon them. No more rumors of wars. Wars all over. India Pakistan, the UK versus the EU. China, North Korea, and Russia invade southeast Asia as the US and its allies respond by bombing their major cities. It's no wonder the good reverend's old flock is pleading for his return to steady the ship in their small town in southern Georgia.

And so it was that Pastor Jones returned to Peachbush to prepare his old flock to survive Armageddon which was erupting all around them in personal as well as public life. The marriage enrichment group which had become a breeding ground for divorce had been disbanded. The church was being sued by two board members for cancelling the annual financial report, which was to have explained why the building fund had been transferred to an unlisted island account somewhere in the Caribbean.

***

<u>Sierra Club news newsletter</u>.

We're Moving On

In conjunction with a wide variety of other humanitarian and religious organizations the Sierra Club is closing down. Founded by John Muir in 1892 to preserve the Yosemite valley as a national park we are moving on. We have abandoned efforts to save whales and wallabies, our precious national forests, and promote clean air and water legislature. All these noble efforts which you, our readers, have supported over the years, must be laid down in order to confront Climate Change. Wildfires in the west; hurricanes and flooding in the east and Gulf states. Tornados, heat waves and droughts in middle America. Half of Long Island under water. Average winter temperature in Canada between 50 and 60 degrees. Alligators, anacondas, lizards and other swampland creatures are creeping, crawling, and wriggling out of the Everglades searching for food and a safe environment.

Along with three hundred and fifty other organizations Sierra Club has joined CCC, Change Climate Change, centered in Berne, Switzerland.

In parting the editors and reporters at Sierra Club want to thank our faithful members for past service, and invite you to join us as we increase our efforts challenging the economic, governmental, and cultural forces that profited from, or have ignored, the pending global suicide. Our neck is in the noose, the chair is shaky. Don't jump.

If you support Sierra Club values you can visit CCC's website at cccworldwide.com for updated information on how you can contribute to Changing Climate Change.

CHAPTER 2

FREE AT LAST

Free at last, free at last. Thank God Almighty I'm free at last. Grinning gleefully to himself Bob Williams, a long term American visitor to Rome from Albuquerque New Mexico, enjoyed the physical bumps and verbal exchanges as he slowly moved through a jumble of elbows, arms, backs, and butts, toward the far wall of the Sistine Chapel. slightly out of breath, Bob gazed up at Michelangelo's Creator reaching out to touch Adam into life on the high ceiling above. Bit redundant; a high ceiling would be above wouldn't it? And no bit; either it's redundant or it's not. Minor idiosyncrasies but Bob enjoyed word play as long as it didn't...

Woof.

Visiting Michelangelo's ceiling every two weeks, wearing his double mask under the Go Lobos baseball cap he'd worn since...

Woof.

and pondered Michelangelo's vision of our groaning creation. A grandiose hallucination someone called it. No landscape, no nature, no tenderness, nothing but huge symbolic bodies floating in space.

Bob saw things differently. It was his Disney World, the playground of the mind that revived his worn and wary soul. On the orthodox side there were the major Old Testament biblical events parading down the long central ceiling: God separating Light from Darkness, the Flood, and Jonah and the whale - both of which reminded him of Carl Jung's watery Unconscious, drunken Noah repenting his sin, and the old man Jeremiah burying his bearded face in his huge hands grieving over the sins of his fellow Jews. On the humanistic side there were the twenty naked young men - ignudi – scattered across the ceiling intruding upon the biblical narrative.

Perhaps Michelangelo had been gay. No clear evidence either way. Catholics like Sister Wendy, the celebrated art historian, think not claiming his loving relationship with Tommaso de'Cavaliere was deep but Platonic. Brushing aside contemporary interest in Michelangelo's sexuality, Bob sat amazed week after week gazing up at the sheer energy and mystical wisdom radiating from the ceiling overhead. Overhead? Yes it was over his head and he could only...

Woof.

The monumental nakedness of the central figures, the rosy bottom of a retreating male figure and the image of Eve crouched suspiciously low in proximity to Adam's genitals had been disturbing at first but as time passed Bob had made peace with his own human nature.

Tilting his head forward to rest his sore neck Bob pondered what he'd seen. This is who we are. Who I am! Shorn of the surrounding buzz of dates and duties that's my soul up there on the ceiling. All my thoughts, my longings, my doubts, my aspirations, my faith are mirrored above. And through it all my radiant Savior opens my heart to the unspeakable goodness that enlivens our groaning creation.

As he walked back through the thinning late afternoon crowd to his everyday world Bob remembered Denise Levertov's, the English born American poet's response to the criticism of the deity as Michelangelo's muscular an old man with a beard. "Not one is a willed fiction. Not one image of God is a lie, but each one; Giotto, Rembrandt, and Michelangelo convey to us the exact manifestation of the Holy One."

***

On his way to his first class from his home on Faculty Row to Harriet Tubman Hall for his first class professor Hank Hangover was. Hungover. Normally a light drinker, switching from white wine to Sidecars half way through Haverford College's traditional first night of the fall semester faculty party was probably unwise, but inhaling deeply professor Hank looked up at the trees lining Faculty Row and smiled. Bright Sky and Deep Roots. Someday he'd weave that thought into one of his lectures, but now he was focused on…

Woof.

He smiled again, puzzled by the secluded little legged low bellied sausage hound, Schatzie who interrupted his musings from time to time; just as Jesus had for so many years. God to dog. And dog back to God? Coincidence? I wonder.

In any event professor Hank loved trees. Mountains and meadows, rivers and roses, shivering oceans and sandy shores, a New Jersey skimmer motionlessly trailing its red beak half a mile in the still bay waters of the nature preserve at the south end of Long Beach Island lit up his day, but trees were special. Bright sky above, deep roots below and, in between, trees. Towering trees, hovering over giraffes and seven foot NBA superstars, soaking up deadly carbon dioxide; exhaling life-giving oxygen, each tree had its own unrepeatable pattern of scaly branches and green. The sturdy cone-shaped evergreens had kept company with giant flying reptiles and grass-eating dinosaurs; quirky conifers whose flowering branches were a wonderland of odd angles that drew Hank's attention just as kaleidoscopic clothed holiday travelers did in a crowded airport. Except that travelers babble on in a variety of languages which sometimes brings them together and often keeps them apart. Strangers in one family. Trees speak an oddly accessible language which embraced Hank every time he was outdoors. "Welcome. We're glad you noticed us. We wish you well." Not in words but sensed. An under-language that reminded Hank of Quaker founder George Fox's reply to a friend who asked why he was smiling after listening to an Indian chief's hour long untranslatable teaching. "I love to hear where words come from." As he'd grown older Hank learned to listen more closely to where his students' words were coming from.

***

Meanwhile in Peachbush, also known locally as Preachbush in honor of Pastor Jones, fifteen year old Jehosphaphat Corrie was falling in love with Sam, rabbi and mizz Cohen's sixteen year old only child. Caught in the sticky web of southern homophobia Hossie and Sam were unable to account for the tender feelings that underlay their earlier guilty rush to relief. The tingly orgasmic adolescent body that invaded their childhood bodies had left them stuck in neutral, motor running but afraid to move into drive for fear of being run down by the Lily White Church in the Valley and Sam's Reform synagogue Tikkun Olan, "Repair the World", which had yet to embrace biblical abominations, and of course their fellow 9th graders who were mercilessly taunting the two fairies.

The two young lads parted awkwardly. Sam asked several nice Jewish girls to the first school dance of the year, but there were no takers, while Hossie who'd cleaned out Walgreen's of chocolate almond Hersey bars and put on fifteen pounds never even tried. Finally the adult Corries and Cohens, who'd moved to the left since Pastor Jones had departed from and returned to the Lily White Church in the Valley supported the lads as best they could. But it was George Bliss a young pastor from Savannah who turned the tide. When the question of "fooling around after dark" came up in Hossie's Sunday school class Pastor Bliss, filling in for deacon Smelly Kelly, said the word was masturbation; that 99 out of a hundred boys did it and the other one's a liar.

Wow! That shook things up in the little old church in the valley, and in the fallout from Pastor Bliss's off the cuff, whatever that means, comments interest in the Hossie-Sam abomination died down the two lads gradually resumed their friendship. To celebrate the coming of age on Sam's sixteenth birthday the Corries and Cohens drove up to Atlanta on Saturday to watch the Braves sweep the Phillies on their way to the World Series. On Sunday they marched in the annual Gay Pride parade, where rabbi Cohen's yarmulke and Hossie and Sam's relationship as the youngest openly gay couple in the parade was featured in the society section of the *Atlantic Journal.* Not to worry; no one in Peachbush ever reads the libelous liberal Journal.

***

"Fair and sunny for the next three days. The weekend should bring heavy showers tapering off in the early part of next week."

***

Looking out my window asdf/ ;lkj the quick brown fox jumped over the lazy dog despite rising ocean levels, forest fires, and hurricanes I can still see the Sandia mountains, watermelon rosy at sunset. The bright sky is still blue; clouds still materialize out of thin air, fade and reemerge in fanciful configurations fresh from God's imagination; the unseen roots of the sun speckled sycamore outside my window are still grounded in the deep earth. The planet changes but persists.

"Why Lord" I'd asked on retreat decades ago, "are the dying autumn leaves so varied, so breath-taking, so beautiful."

"All to please you John."

Dorothy Day quoting Dostoevsky wrote that beauty will save the world. Every day I wake up to wonders around me. Everyday my endangered planet brings me the comforting embrace of....

Wuff. Wuff.

***

"Darling?"

"Yes dear?"

"Faster faster I love you."

"O God. O God I'm cuming."

***

"This is Wiggy Shlossenmeir bringing you what's happening in the world today from WPAX Berne, Switzerland. In breaking news the pandemic in the US shows signs of leveling off as 82% of the population have now been vaccinated. The Republican Trump inspired governor's recall effort in California fell far short as Governor Newson again won two thirds of the popular vote. Bad news for Republicans in the 2022 midterms. The Supreme Court has ruled 5 to 4 that president Trump must testify under oath on all his financial documents dating from 2012. Here at home Chanel No 5 won the coveted contract to deodorize the smelly Berne bears. In Swiss politics president Roger Federer has won the Nobel Prize for his work in Africa promoting reconciliation between warring factions in Kenya by introducing grassroots tennis and yodeling. In sports at age 42 Roger, having defeated Nadal in the French Open and Djokovic in the US Open is being acclaimed as the greatest men's tennis player of all time. In US sports the Philadelphia Eagles beat the Dallas Cowboys 59-3, to advance to the Super Bowl."

CHAPTER 3

THE CLOUD OF KNOWING

Fox News.

"Pastor Jones, what can you tell our listeners about your visit with president Trump?"

"He was cordial, he listened he…"

"I understand you spoke extensively of Armageddon. Can you tell us the president's response?"

"The president agreed we were living through the last days."

"Can you be more specific?"

"Long Island under water. The Atlantic coastline from Maine to Florida flooded inland for forty miles. The UK driven out of London by the EU as far north as the Midlands. Pakistan threatening the Taj Mahal with WMD unless India…"

Woof.

"And it's your view Pastor Jones we're in the midst of the Last Days?"

"Yes. You've only to look at….""

Arf.

***

New York Times Editorial

Yogi Was Right

In these difficult times it's refreshing to remember New York's own guru, Yogi Barra's challenging words. "It aint over till it's over." Down four runs in the ninth with the top of the order yet to bat there's still hope. First: the UN has made progress in the Middle East negotiating a ceasefire between Iran and Turkey, Finland and New Zealand have signed a No Nukes treaty, and India and Pakistan are holding peace talks in Delhi. Pope Philip Neri's climate change conference opened today in the Vatican, while firefighters, the military and concerned citizens are being mobilized around the world to erect levees and flood walls to hold back rising oceans levels from flooding the costal countries. Social workers are helping the disposed find replacement homes in…

Woof.

All these desperate measures are necessitated of course by Trump-minded nationalistic leaders around the globe who refuse to listen to the environmental scientists. When religion ignores reason the results can be horrendous. And it all could have been avoided if only…

Woof.

But as Yogi said, "it ain't over till it's over." Hang in there America. Help is on the way.

***

"I blame the Communists. It all started when Putin…

"It's the 1% fat cats who knew a good thing when they saw it. The big flood prevention companies: FCA – Flood Control of America, Flood Protection Barriers, Big Bags…"

"Don't forget the Army of Engineers. Lot of money going down that rat hole."

"With rats in and out of government waiting for the cheese to drip down from above."

"You can't believe anything you hear, Harry. But mark my words. Follow the money and you'll …."

Ruff.

***

Friends Journal

Speaking Truth to Trump

It's not the liberals Mr. President. Forget the Deep State. It didn't start with your losing the election in 2020. Forget Armageddon. How it started, who's to blame, is not the question. The question is what can you do to save the country. First of course levees and sea walls (not the same) must be put in place to preserve dry America, A second major…

Woof.

***

EWTN Your Pro-life Catholic News Channel reminds our listeners that despite the flooding along a narrow stretch of coastal land, which Trump has well in hand, our major moral issue is still the heartless killing of unborn babies. As we have in the past EWTN urges our pro-life listeners to bombard the Vatican with….

Wau. Wau.

***

"Proud Boys!"

"Proud Boys!"

"Proud Boys!"

"Settle down."

"Proud Boys. Proud…"

"Shut up! Shut the fuck up. I got news."

Quiet.

"QAon is calling for a rally in Boise on New Year's Eve. They'll do the organizing. We in?"

[Short discussion]

"Those opposed?"

Silence.

"The motion passes. We're going to Boise."

Small talk on what a great town Boise is. No masks, no vaccines, lotta Trumpsters. Cold as fuckin' hell. Bikes welcome. Etc."

"Whatta they want from us?"

"Snipers. Two snipers."

"Snipers?"

"Whoa. Fuckin' shit that's..."

"It's Armageddon Jack. Blood will flow."

"I dunno. Armageddon's a crock."

"Jack's right we gotta a more specific agenda. Pick off the fuckin' Snowflakes and take charge when chaos subsides. Preserve Western culture. No jungle bunny hip hop. No spicking Spanish. English. One language, one country the way it was. The way it should be."

"The way it fuckin'g will be."

"Amen brother."

"Fuck Armageddon. 'Member Reggie telling the mayor of Portland. 'I'm comin' for ya, ya little punk. Your days are fuckin'g numbered.'"

"An' Joe Briggs's 'It's time for war if they steal this shit. Lettum die a traitors death.'"

"Yeah Joe got it right. That's our shtick."

"The rest of you ok with snipers?"

Nods.

"I still think..."

"Yeah fuckin'g shit I agree with...."

"Don't think assholes, it's time to move. We talk big. Now's the time to act big... And Jack? Ace? Don't think 'bout leaving the group. Right?"

Pause.

"Right."

"Right."

***

"Gentle Reader?"

"What?"

"What's your view? You've heard the options. Armageddon. Save the unborn. It's the communist Democrats. It's the 1% fat cats farting on the rest of us; especially the poor. Get out the vote. Storm the capital. Raise hell, take back our nation. Pray. Peace marches. Fasting. Support the young people. The UN. Trump's the problem. Trump's the solution. Snippers. What's your view gentle reader?"

"Why drag me in? You've already got your own solution."

"No really. I don't."

"Then why bring it up?"

"I do have a suggestion."

"Ah."

"Remember *The Cloud of Unknowing*?"

"A bit. A no-name medieval mystic argues the sovereign source, God, is beyond human knowledge. Which in this case is you as the author. You're writing the book so everyone's in the dark but you."

"I could claim author's privilege."

"But you won't. Why not?"

"Because I don't know either. I'm in my own cloud of left-wing politics, Quaker pacifism, and Vatican II Catholicism.

"So that's as far as we can go? Everyone lives out their most compelling response to St. Paul's groaning creation? To climate change; to the silent plague that moves unseen air between us; wars; torture; economic, racial and gender injustice and…"

WOOF!

"I wasn't done."

WOOF!

CHAPTER 4

NETWORKING

Evening star up yonder teach me like you to wander
Willing and obediently the path that God ordains for me.
Teach me gentle flowers to wait for springtime showers;
in this winter world to grow green and strong beneath the snow.

Settling into silence in the side chapel at the abbey fifteen Norbertine brothers and two sisters waited on abbot Joel's Advent homily. After touching on the Christmas Star by night, abbot Joel deftly shifted to the Light by day warming the dark earth that meadows, crops and trees might flourish. Just as the abbot was moving into the Light Within Father Andrew was drifting away from Joel's sermon to the *Cosmic Love Song* he'd written while spending a week visiting Margie, his younger sister, a social worker at Kewa Pueblo formerly known as Santa Domingo Pueblo Indian Reservation forty miles north of Albuquerque on the highway to...

Arf..... the song dammit...... Woof."

.... *Softening his gaze*[4]

Sun lays a warm and healing hand

---

[4] Author's poem.

Upon his lover's naked breast;
As seas receive his fiery seed.
How gently his light kisses fall upon his lover's lips.
See how he fills her flesh discreetly
Till plants thrill and throb with green.
See the languid meadow open to the wanton sky.
Listen to the whispered love words
Pass tween Gaia and the Sun.
Mountains moaning stretch to sunlight.
Rivers run to writhing sea.
The earth alive with ecstasy.

"Let light Lord enter me"
Bursting from translucent waters;
Pleads from every leafy tree.
Listen to the biosphere bending into burning sun.
"Let light Lord enter me."
Iiiiiii YaH Iiiiiii YaH Iiiiii YaH Iiiiiiiiiii

Turning as the Sun sinks westward into arms of sleepy night
Gaia whispers to her lover
"Let your dark light cover me."
Oyyyyya Oyyyyyyya Oyyyyyyya hoooooommm
"Let your dark light cover me."

"Father Andrew. Father Andrew. We're waiting; it's your turn."
"What?"
"It's your turn. The wine."

***

"Mothafucker. Shut up. Just shut the fuck up."

"Who you telling to shut up mothafucker. You're goin' to Boise. Ace too."

"Hey man. It's a free world. Gimme one good reason we gotta go. I'm broke. The bike's in the shop."

"To keep you mothafuckers close. We don't trust you. OK… You're goin'. We checked on your fuckin' bike. It's fine. We'll get you money. You two can sleep on the floor in Tarrios's room. He'll keep a fuckin' eye on you."

***

Sara Snoop, formerly investigative reporter for the Haverford Herald now anchorwoman for public television WPBS Berne grinned from ear to ear. Well not quite from…

Woof.

But she was pleased. In ten minutes she'd be on air moderating her first big interview. Between Pastor Jones of the Lily White Church in the Valley in Peachbush Georgia and Father Andrew, ex-pickpocket, now a Norbertine priest from Daylesford Abbey in suburban Philadelphia.

"Pastor Jones you see humanity as an endangered species…"

"More than endangered Sara dear. You, I, Father Andrew, and those listening are living in the last days. *Revelation 14: 19-20* says *"The angel swung his sickle over the earth… and blood flowed as high as a horse's bridle."* Given the summer long riots, looting, and violence against the police in our major cities and widespread wars overseas I think you'll agree *Revelation's* prophecy has come to pass.

I leave aside references to Father Andrew's church. Well just one. *"Babylon – Rome - the great mother of whores and the earth abominations." Revelation 17: 5*. Physically and spiritually chaos reigns."

"Spiritually Pastor Jones?"

"Woe to the earth and the sea for the devil has come down to you with great wrath." Rev. 12-12.

Whoa. Quite a start, Sara reflected, as she turned to Father Andrew for his response.

"Pastor Jones you may be right. I don't think you are; but since the future's not ours to see, you may be right."

Confused by the young Norbertine's response Sara asked Father Andrew if he was agreeing with Pastor Jones.

"O no. Most biblical scholars believe *Revelation* is not a book for the ages but is a contemporary response to the suffering being inflicted on Christians by the Roman Empire. They argue conservative Christians ignore the historical circumstances in which *Revelation* was written."

"Pastor Jones?"

"An old issue Sara between those who place scripture above commentary like myself, and those like Father Andrew who don't."

The two men smiled across the moderator seated between them who had only the barest understanding of the issues that divided the two men. Historically, theologically, and culturally.

"Father Andrew?"

"We both agree St. Paul's 'groaning creation' is an apt phrase to describe the situation we face. My view of God's coming Kingdom of God on earth as good news is far less dire than Pastor Jones. The Lord's prayer says whoever does God's will is part of the kingdom of heaven come down to earth. Not 'Lord, Lord' Christians but 'peacemakers' who 'hunger and thirst for righteousness', as the heretical good Samaritan..."

"Father Andrew?"

"Yes Pastor Jones?"

"The gospel is now. The now Jesus lived in is long past. Your own liberal Albert Schweitzer called the Sermon on the Mount an interim ethic that leads us into the Last Days."

"Father Andrew?"

"Yes Sara?"

Pause.

"You said Pastor Jones might be right about God's wrathful day of Judgement. Doesn't that worry you? Nonbelievers cast into the lake of eternal fire. Tortured forever."

"I don't believe that."

"But that's what the Bible says."

"The bible says many things. Written over two thousand years by devout but fallible human historians, scribes, and prophets facing a variety of challenges scripture is..."

"Like a shopping mall? Pick and choose what you like?"

"Sounds like you two have been doing that for the last twenty five minutes. Since our time is almost up what final word would you like to leave with our listeners? You first Pastor Jones."

"We've moved on from Christ's interim ethics into the Last Days; when God is separating sheep from goats. Get on board; chaos is coming back. Won't be water but fire this time. Perhaps nuclear fire."

"Father Andrew?"

"It doesn't matter who's right about how the world ends. That's descriptive truth. And we both agree the planet is threatened by a host of problems; physically - and spiritually which we haven't touched on yet. What matters is how we respond to the crisises we face."

"Thank you Pastor Jones, Father Andrew. This is Sara Snoop. Be sure to tune in next week when our guests be..."

Off air the discussion continued.

"... Descriptive truth describes the situation. It's chained to the past. Prescriptive truth does not describe the situation; it's about the future. It responds to the situation. Prescriptive truth is ethical; it's about making choices into the future. Have we family and friends who need our help? What's our response to the pandemic? To climate change? To poverty, racism, and the endless appeals to support violence against our enemies. *Revelation* says 'if you kill with the sword you must be killed.' Bit harsh but..."

"I never rejected the teachings of Jesus. I just said liberals reject and mock, our Lord and Savior Jesus Christ the Son of God and our salvation."

"Sadly many do, but the test is not what they say Pastor Jones but what they do. You for example believe the church I represent is the whore of Babylon, the cause of all our present problems, yet you call me Father Andrew and treat me with respect as we discuss our differences."

***

It's all about networking. Connecting with folks who have a burning concern in at least one common area of interest. .

***

Onward Christian Soljers marching as to war with the cross of...

"Hello. This is Pastor Jones of God's Lily White
Church in the Valley."

"My name's Enrique Tarrio."

"I'm afraid we don't do business with the Proud Boy's Mr. Tarrio."

"Hear me out."

"Yes?"

"I think we have overlapping interests in bringing down the fuckin' government."

"Go on."

"We're helping promote a rally in Boise in two weeks. TBA. Take Back America. We'll like you to promote the event among your followers; or at least refrain from denouncing it."

"I'm afraid I can't support such an event."

"Look you asshole we're on the same side. We hate Democrats; you hate the mothafuckin' Democrats. We gotta take back our country."

"Too late. Amageddon's already underway."

"Whatever. The point is we both want to screw the liberals."

Pause.

"I'll call you back, Mr. Tarrio."

***

"President Foxxy?"

"Ex-president Foxxy but go on."

"This is Mr. Tarrio from the Proud Boys."

"I've heard the name. Go on."

"We're helpin' organize the Take Back America rally in Boise in a coupla weeks and we'd like your support."

"You do know I'm an ex college president for a reason. Presently I'm serving time in the state penitentiary in Philadelphia. You sure I'm what you want to promote your event?"

"Not publically, but you have contacts that could be useful to us. The Coast-to-Coast trucking company for one. And Tim Rottenburger, a budding T.V. anchorman who's being interviewed on CBS next Sunday as the voice of pissed off young libertarians."

"What's in for me?"

"Half a million to get you started when you get out."

"I'll see what I can do."

"You have my number. I need a response by Friday."

Click.

***

Joyful Joyful we adore thee God of...

"Bob?"

"Yes Joel."

Bob Williams from Albuquerque, now pope Philip Neri and abbot Joel from Daylesford Norbertine abbey in...

Ruff, ruff. Arf!

are on the phone. The pope in Rome; the abbot in Pennsylvania have been friends since their days together studying for the priesthood at Villanova. Their conversation opens with three minutes of small talk. The pope's family back in Albuquerque will miss him at Christmas. His favorite nephew is studying environmental ethics at Swarthmore, Aunt Eileen has the virus and is on a ventilator in downtown Presbyterian. His mom and dad are settling into La Vida Llena, a retirement community where dad plays poker and leads a Listening to the Inner Voice of Love group, while mom does pottery and attends movies and lectures.

Joel's surviving older sister, Marge, the social worker on the reservation has been adopted into Kewa Pueblo, formerly known as Pueblo Nation at Santa Domingo. The chief sends his prayers for the church and the world. He appreciates the pope's Mass celebrating the founding of Kewa Pueblo which though recognized by the Spanish in 1600 has been living on the same land for thousands of years. Father Andrew's friends in the liberal Last Chance Pentecostal Church and St. Mick's in Atlantic City are fine.

"And the abbey?"

"Father Andrew has been in touch with Berne and Father Lopez and the Corries in Peachbush."

"And?"

"The consensus is we need to keep an eye on the Proud Boy's involvement in the Boise rally next week. Andrew and I will be attending..."

"Send someone else. You two have been seen on the telly."

"And Hossie..."

"Corrie. Same problem."

"We'll find someone."

"Keep me posted. We also have people in place. We'll need many open ears if we're to prevent more violence."

"You think Boise's a real threat? Could be just another alt-right rally. Trump's not attending and he hasn't given it his support."

"Not publically but behind the scenes he's putting up the money and lending his expertise in rallying the base. Rumor has it with QAnon and the Proud Boys involved this could be a dangerous event."

***

Standing on the pebbled shore looking out over the never-ending North Atlantic an ecumenical band of Catholic monks, Presbyterians, Anglicans, Lutherans, and a healthy mix of humanists prepare to celebrate the rediscovered Gloria sung by abbot Columba and his monks thirteen hundred years ago in 563 C.E. The abbot and a hearty band of twelve companions had left the isolated lonely isle of Iona, off the northwestern coast of Scotland on a pilgrimage of repentance for Columba's part in promoting violence between fellow Christians. Previously blinded by Walter Winks' "myth of redemptive violence" Columba, a large and physically intimidating man, devoted his life to evangelizing for the Prince of Peace.

Standing on the pebbly shore looking out over the dark shivering waters the ecumenical band were mindful of the ancient abbot's quest to sail in a currach, an Irish long boat covered with animal skins, to evangelize the Picts on the Scotch mainland and farther south down into Briton. Today parishes and churches around the world to honor St. Columba's memory; in words if not always in his courageous quest to follow the truth wherever it might lead. And now Columba's contemporary followers gather on the shore to offer their own hearts, in three rising choruses of praise, to their loving God.

Gloria, Gloria, Gloria, in Excel sis Deo.
Gloria, Gloria, Gloria, in Excel sis Deo.
Gloria, Gloria, Gloria, in Excel sis Deo.

CHAPTER 5

BANG ONE

Boxed faces on the screen include Proud Boys Afro-Cuban chairman Enrique Tarrio[5], Pastor Jones Armageddon organizer, QAnon's Q possibly Ron Watkins, and ex-college president Dr. Sly Foxxy currently in prison in Philadelphia.

[Tarrio] Did you find us a hotel? Nothing fancy; nothing traceable.

[Q] Cabana Boise. Cheapest downtown motel in the city. Three blocks from the Arena.

"I thought we were booking the Bandstand in the park."

"Already taken."

"And the stadium?"

"The Broncos have a home game on our date."

---

[5] Enrique Tarrio, chairman of the Proud Boys (2021) at the time of our story is an Afro-Cuban who points to his ethnicity and the mixed ethnicity of some of his followers as proof he's not a White Supremacist. The judge who sentenced Tarrio to five months in jail for burning BLM flags disagreed. "Mr. Tarrio's conduct express none of the democratic values he claims to have." My interpretations of chairman Tarrio is entirely my own based on the what I know of his participation in the neo-Nazi white supremacy movement and inciting violence to support what he calls White Chauvinism.

"What's the Arena?"

"The Idaho Central Arena. Nothing special but it'll hold most of our crowd. Overflow always looks good on T.V."

"And the motel?"

"Worst in the city. Untraceable. I read the reviews. "A Total Piece of Crap… a disgusting facility. Carpets were black from stains, paint faded and nasty, room smelled terrible. AC did not work." One more. "… As soon as we arrived there were about 12 people, all about 18 to early 20s in the hallway outside our room, all drinking, smoking and being extremely loud. The front desk said they never heard them being loud. This went on till about 3: 30 AM but got much louder once the fighting and screaming started. Someone threatened to use a gun. The front desk said it was just guests having a good time. Finally they did call the cops. About 4:30 one police car came and no one was arrested. Then we checked out."

"Sounds like our kind of place. Did the motel respond?"

"They said and I quote. 'We appreciate you taking time to review us. We apologize your stay was not satisfying and hope you'll give us another try in the near future.'"

Pause.

"So we got the Rally booked and a place to stay. Ron… Sorry. Q. What's the big picture?"

"The Rally will be raucous. We're not talking to middle America here. We're lighting up the base to take action. Our guys are warriors in God's war against Satan. Yours are… "

"Patriots taking back our mothafuckin' country."

Pause.

"You got what I asked for?"

"They're ready. Here?"

"Not here. The rally's just a distraction. I'll let you know later."

"What's the program?"

"Country Rock as the crowd gathers. We open with Onward Christian Soljers, and Grand Old Flag. Then Pastor Jones gives the blessing, someone from Q goes over the basics: first the Great Awakening and then the Storm."

"The what?'

"The Awakening is when sleepy sinners wake up to God's Judgement Day. The Storm is God's Armageddon as the warriors for Christ take up arms – physically - against the Whore of Babylon. The Satan saturated world churches. The Satanic kingdoms of this world. China, Russia, and America, which once held such promise. The darkies and spicks, who are corrupting our Western way of life."

"Good message. Encourages my flock to kick ass, not just mouth off and pray; but it's a bit tricky for me. I can't endorse QAnon publicly. Satanic cannibalistic pedophiles running the U.S. government isn't the way my folks see it. But I can associate our movement with a broad based coalition of diverse groups all working to…"

Grrrr…. Woof!….. grrrrrrrr.

"What was that?"

"Nothing. Let's move on."

"You need a bridge concept. Something to rally diverse groups into a focused movement."

"Take Back America; that's our bridge."

"Not entirely. Most Q folks don't give a shit about taking back the government. America's just part of the problem."

Pause.

"Deep State? Ambiguous enough for QAnon, and political enough for Proud Boys and neo-Nazi groups on the Right."

Pause.

"Not bad. I'll keep it in mind."

"What's next?"

"*Dixie*, God Bless America, a moment of silence for the imprisoned patriots of Jan. 6. Then the Proud Boys, not too long, a disclaimer not to engage in violence, our national anthem and we go for the press conference while the crowd goes to raise hell in the streets. At the Capitol? At the United Vision for Idaho headquarters on West Jefferson St.?"

"Which would have the most impact nationally?"

"Not our problem. We have nothing to do with the crowd after they leave us."

"You mentioned the rally was a distraction. From what?"

"Not your concern Pastor. I'll keep you posted…"

"Right. Well. [sighs] Good meeting. See you all in my room at the Cabana an hour after check in time. 4: 00 next week. Reverend you have a closing prayer?"

"O Lord spare us from the holocaust to come and bless our efforts to serve you on the great day of wrath. Bless QAnon, the Proud Boys, and President Foxxy and his little band at Haverford. May he be released from jail soon. In the name of Jesus, Amen, brothers, Amen."

***

"This is the Big Wig, Wiggy Schlossenmeir, coming to you from station WPAX Berne, Switzerland, welcoming our new viewers in the U.S. and Canada. Locally, president Federer awarded coveted golden tennis racquets to the twelve brave sisters of Our Lady of St. Bernard who scaled the north wall of the Matterhorn in the record time of five hours and fifteen minutes. In news from abroad the US Senate remains deadlocked over president Trump's proposal to privatize the national parks; the chairman, of the US-Canadian committee Save Our Coastlines, has resigned and remains unavailable for comment. In Boise, Idaho police and the National Guard, rife with insurrectionist sympathizers were unable to restore order after the crowd leaving the QAnon sponsored Take Back America rally, headed for the state Capitol brandishing baseball bats, pitchforks, and automatic weapons. A QAnon spokesperson has expressed regret for the violence saying "We deplore the tragic events in Boise. Our only goal is to change minds and hearts in preparation for the coming day of Judgement. In other news..

I've just been handed an update. Former vice-president Pamela Harris who was ahead in the polls for the upcoming presidential election has just been killed by two snipers at her home in California. Details to follow. This is Big Wig Schossenmeir wishing you a pleasant evening from Berne, Switzerland."

CHAPTER 6

RESPONSE TO BANG

"Wiggy?"

"Jawohl, mein president."

"We have to meet. Is ten o'clock tomorrow on Zoom good for you? You don't go to the station till three."

"Ja madam president. Good by me. Who else is coming?"

"The Norbertines: Joel, Andrew and Phyllis; professor Hank, and Schatzi. The dogs elected her as their representatives. Arnold says she'll be fine."

"What about the Peachbush gang? Father Lopez, the Corries and Cohens. St. Peter and Paul here in Berne where the dogs live? St. Mike's and the four Dorothy Day nuns in Atlantic City?"

"Start with a small group and add on."

"Good by me. Anything I can bring?"

"A clear head and a kind heart."

"Auf Wiedershen madam president."

"Ciao."

Click.

***

By 10: 15 the next morning all eight Zoomers were on screen.

"Woof.... .... Woof Woof Arf."

"Arnold. Tell Schatzi she'll have to wait her turn."

"Schatzi?"

Woof?

"....... ....?"

"... ...."

"She says she's sorry and will wait her turn."

"We all here?"

Pause.

"Anyone not here please raise..."

"Ruff!"

"Good. You all know the problem we face. The QAnon rally in Boise left seven Capitol police and fifteen anti-protesters seriously wounded. Two fatalities. Thank God the bomb truck was stopped in time but it was a blood bath. And a diversion from the two snipers who killed Pamela Harris, the likely Democratic candidate running against Trump in November."

"Why two?"

"I'm not sure."

"Backup in case one missed?"

"These are desperate men. And the apparent rapprochement..."

Woof? ....?

"Schatzi says what's rapprochement."

"Bringing two hostile groups together. The marriage between the secular *Take Back America* Proud Boys and the QAnon's Armageddon fanatics is scary. Ideas?"

"Investigate Trump's connection to the violence."

"More security at public events."

"Non-violent demonstrations. A peace pledge to report..."

"We need more information. We need to know their plans. We need a mole."

"Or a dog?"

***

Conference call.

"We need a living logo. Something people can relate to. After Boise we need to soften our fuckin' image. I told the media we were in Boise not California. We don't know nothin' bout the shooting, but rumors are flyin'... Jack look it up on the fuckin' internet. Penguins, Koala bears, anything fuckin' cute."

***

"Arnold? Arnold Really O'Reilly."

"Yes?"

"You have a dachshund?"

"Who is this?"

"A friend who wants to warn you about the Proud Boys' plan to dynamite the Capitol."

Pause.

Big sigh. Whoa!

"I'm listening."

"I don't know when, but they're looking for something cute to deflect attention away from their image as a terrorist gang."

"But they are a terrorist gang. You just said they plan to blow up the Capitol..."

"Not in their own name. We learned that after January 6th. Too many Proud Boys went to jail or recanted for a lesser sentence."

"Why not call the..."

"Listen shithead you wanta stop the bomb or not? I don't trust the fuckin' government."

"O right. Tell me what I need to do."

"Take your fuckin' dog to Boise. Next Thursday at 3:00 check in at the Cabana Boise and sit by the desk. When I come in with three or four rough dudes get up and leave with the dog."

"Where?"

"To your room. Just make sure the dog is seen. I'll do the rest. My name's Jack. I'm a big guy. Red hair. Scar on my left cheek; snake tattoos on both arms, but you never saw me before. And the Cabana's a real dump so dress accordingly. Don't shave. You're pissed off at the fuckin' government. You're looking for action. You served four years in the sandbox. Don't use your right name. Nobody does. You were busted for drugs somewhere back east."

"That's not me."

Pause.

"I've got a friend who was busted for…"

"Send him. And the dog. Gotta go."

Click.

***

Back against the leather seat back, knees cramped against the seat in front, Bob Williams stretched his shoulders and looked out the window waiting for take-off to Albuquerque by way of Dallas. Double-masked under his old UNM cap, Bob Williams closed his eyes and drifted into inner conversation with Schatzi.

"'A *Wendy's* big bacon cheeseburger and Coke before morning classes; green chili chowder and so papilla at the *Frontier* before afternoon classes weren't common events. Most of the time I ate canned baked beans and ketchup, or grilled cheese and Campbell's tomato soup with my roommates: Milspaugh, the dancing bear at our Saturday night keg parties, now with IBM; Norrie the scholar who read the required reading three times and graduated Cum Lauda, now with…"

"Woof."

"… *La Crepe Michel* in Old Town when I was dating an exchange student, Juliette Piaf, from Paris."

"Woof?"

"Not related."

"Ruff? Ruff?"

"Yes we were in a relationship."

"…… ………?"

"Three years. Juliette was the love of my life. Short, dark hair with bangs and dark eyes that listened before she spoke. A beautiful young woman, with a slight lisp when she spoke English. She was a painter; loved Van Gogh especially the early Van Gogh, and the German Expressionists. An ardent Marxist. She married a Dane, a Special Ed teacher in an underfunded middle school that catered to the forgotten waifs of Paris…"

"Woof?.... .... ?"

"We keep in touch. She has three kids and I'm still a bachelor. The last time we talked she..."

***

Editor author conversation.

"John?"

"Yes?"

"Why are we wasting time with Bob Williams, (also known as Pope Philip Neri) in New Mexico when all the action takes place in Berne, Rome, and the east coast?"

Pause.

"Because Bob's a special person as you might have guessed by now. Because the seemingly irrelevant bits of ordinary life stabilizes our riveting drama where the 'fate of the planet hangs in the balance' whatever that means. And because a story line without independent characters is contrived. Of course they want to wander away from the plot and make the story all about me. My life my struggles. Of course characters want to be in charge."

"But John you're the author. It's your job to keep things moving."

"I know that but I need the characters. I can do the plot; just make an outline: present the problem, introduce the characters, several failed attempts to solve the problem and an unexpected ending that will satisfy at least a majority of the readers.

Real characters communicate with the author who does have the last word, but without their input..."

Woof!

"What's Bob Williams like? What's he thinking when his plane bumps down in Albuquerque?"

New Mexico, New Mexico we sing to honor thee.

The golden haze of college days will live in memory.

This praise we sing will ever ring

With truth and loyalty.

New Mexico your fame we know will last eternally...

"Perhaps not eternally but it's lasted forty years while I had my moment with God which sent me to seminary and eventually Rome...

Hail to thee New Mexico we pledge our faith to thee,
Fighting ever, yielding never.
HAIL! HAIL! HAIL!
"Bit tacky; but not bad for a start.
ALLELUIA! ALLELUIA! ALLELUIA!

***

Proud Boy chairman Enrique Tarrio bangs on the motel bell. Gino a short man in his 60's wiping his large mouth with a ugly orange handkerchief comes out from the back.

"How may I help you gentleman?"

"We have reservations for four under Brando."

Gino looks it up.

"Room 125 and126."

"Thanks."

As Mr. Brando turns to go he notices a rough dude, with an unleashed black and tan long dog, getting up from the one under-stuffed chair in the small check-in room and heading for the door. The dog hangs back turning toward Mr. Brando with a wistful look.

"Nice dog you got there."

"What's it to you. He'll not for sale."

The dog follows his master strapped with a shabby canvas backpack, who heads for their motel room. Street level 101.

Ten minute pause.

Knock. Knock.

"Who's there?"

"Guys you don't wanta mess with."

"Fuck off. I'm busy."

"Open the fuckin' door or we'll be waiting for you outside."

The door opens onto a sparse, untidy motel room; half empty Jack Daniels bottle and shot glass by the unmade bed; rumpled patched Levis tossed over a chair; twenty four inch Emerson T.V. in the corner with an "out of order" note pasted to the dusty glass screen. Mr. Brando takes one of the chairs and motions for the dog owner in his blue boxer shorts to take the other.

"You heard of the Proud Boys?"

The rough dude's eyes brighten briefly.

"Go on."

"We want your dog as our living logo."

"Your what?'

"We put your fuckin' cute dog on social media, T shirts, billboards. You get a hundred grand."

Rough dude's eyes remain steady.

Pause.

"The dog don't relate to strangers."

The discussion goes on for another ten minutes as the details are worked out and it's agreed Marlo, as he prefers to be called, will encourage Woof to work for the Proud Boys, but after working hours he and Woof are to be left alone.

"The money's no good if I can't spend it in peace."

Mr. Brando sits back and agrees, with no intention of not keeping tabs on his two unidentified coconspirators.

***

"Good evening and welcome to Tucker Carlson, the most watched T.V. news show in America. Tonight I'll be interviewing three special guests. Two men and a dog. The men are Enrique Tarrio, Afro-Cuban chairman of the Proud Boys, a proud organizer and spokesperson for patriotic Americans who would disrupt the Democrats Marxist agenda. My other guests are Woof, a low bellied long dog, and his trainer, who calls himself Marlo. Marlo let me start with you. How did you and Schatzi first meet?"

"First, thanks for having us on Tucker. I met Schatzi in a lost dog shelter. While the other dogs were yipping and yapping to attract my attention Woof was lying on the soiled sawdust floor in her crowded cage, wheezing and coughing, gasping for breath. When I asked the owner why she wasn't being treated he said "O she'll be dead in two hours. We have to care for the healthy ones first."

"And you've cared for her ever since. Very commendable.... Enrique what attracted you to Schatzi?"

"The Proud Boys were looking for a spokesperson to represent our patriotic movement to take back America, but no eagles, no cougars. No animals with attitude. Something softer and when I saw Schatz I knew this was the one. Dachshunds were bred three hundred years ago in Germany to hunt badgers to their hidden holes; they were also affectionate animals. Especially with children. Fierce to pursue their enemies. Friendly to cuddle with small children on the couch."

"Woof, Woof....... ...." and with that Woof trotted on her little legs across the stage and jumped into Carlson Tucker's lap and went to sleep.

Pause for applause.

"Any last words for our audience Enrique?"

"I hope our interview inspires your audience of patriots to not be afraid to rid our world of badgers who hide in dark holes. And I hope it nurtures love of country, and one another, which is at the heart of our movement."

***

Somewhere there's a seashore where the wind is blowing free
And the wheeling gulls above evoke the music of the sea.
Somewhere there's a hillside, where you can climb at dawn,
And wonder at the sunrise as another day is born.

***

Anderson Cooper CNN host.

"Good evening. In about eighteen hours Senate minority leader Mitch McConnell will be meeting with his Republican colleagues known as The Block, but we begin tonight with an unusual guest. Schatzi is a dashing badger hunting dachshund who has brought with him his proud owner Enrique Tarrio chairman of the Proud Boys. Enrique is seen by many as a true patriot not afraid to take on the "Deep State" by direct action.

We also invited his trainer, deacon Lance Lott from Berne whose views differ from Enrique's and the Proud Boys. We begin with Enrique."

"Thank you for having me on Anderson."

After several minutes of light humor between Tarrio and his trainer about their different political views Tarrio, a powerfully build unshaven Afro-Cuban with penetrating dark eyes, settles into his expose of the Deep State that underlies the façade of constitutional governments around the world. Sounding like the socialist senator from Vermont Tarrio castigates the new 1% robber barons, who siphon off 40% of the national wealth while his people – whites, rich and poor - who built this country – are dismissed as ignorant bigots.

"Which some of them are. Several years ago in Charleston, South Caroline I remember hearing a torch carrying crowd chanting 'Jews will not replace..."

"Fuck you Anderson. I didn't come on your show to make nice."

"Then why not join the Bernie Sanders's crowd to get fat cats like me from eating all the cat food?"

"Because" Lance cut in "the Proud Boys are interested in violence not relieving poverty."

"Because Anderson, patriotic Americans resent the foreigners who've taken over our culture."

"But you do have a common enemy. The Proud Boys like other Alt-Right groups have cut ties to their one-time messiah, Trump, because..."

"He didn't follow through. He started well with the..."

WOOF.

Pause.

"I see you've brought a guest of your own. Lance can tell us what he brings to the table."

"She Anderson. Sadly like too many Americans living in poverty Schatzi can't reach the table. But I'd like to..."

"Anderson, can we get back to Schatzi and the Proud Boys?"

After an awkward pause Anderson nods and

Enrique continues.

"Schatzi represents the soft side of our movement. We're not just badger hunters; we're ordinary hardworking Americans who love our country and love one another. Schatzi represents this..."

Woof.

"What's she want?"

"I think she wants to talk to your audience. Schatzi? Go ahead."

"..... .. .. arf....... .... woff..... Bow Wow...... ...."

"Thank you Schatzi. That's enough."

*WOOF...... ....###****@@%%%%%#####......*

"I said that's enough."

"####!!!!))))%%%%%% QQQQ @@@@@..."

"Shut up you fuckin' dog. Shut the fuck up."

"Enrique! Enrique sit down."

ZZZZZZpppppp.

As Enrique stumbles and slips to the polished stage floor chasing Schatzi, the plain clothes cop who'd been waiting in the wings in case there was an incident bends over and removes the tranquilizer dart that had put a stop to the impending chaos. Anderson Cooper, cool as ever, invites his viewers to stay tuned at the top of the hour for expert commentary on the bizarre events they'd all witnessed on the Anderson Cooper show on CNN America's No. 1 source for news.

CHAPTER 7

TWO CLOUDS

What's the capital of Poland?

How late is the nearest Walgreens open?

Who are the Oath Keepers?

Where can I get good green chili in Minneapolis?

... evening Yoga classes in...

Was Michelangelo gay?

Will Trump seek a third term?

Is the pope liberal or conservative?

... has the latest vaccine virusbegone.com been approved by...?

... recipe for Cajan Lobster Newburgh...

Do Unitarians believe in God?

Which Vatican II Catholic church in San Francisco has the best childcare?

... best travel value for an elderly couple visiting Greece for two weeks....

What's the most bible-based Protestant church near me?

Is there a God?

Yes. God's name is Google. It lives on high in the Cloud. Google is all-knowing. Google is all-powerful. Google translates the blooming buzzing confusion around you into words and ideas to live by. Google is based on facts, not poopy personal opinions. Google is way smarter than you. Google cares about you. Whoever you may be; whatever your race, religion, income level, I.Q., gender, age, or political persuasion, Google speaks to your needs directly. Occasionally Google seems to contradict itself, but let that go; Google is way smarter than you and can be trusted to provide all the support you need to live a productive and prosperous life.

What should I do with my life?

Read my book. Go to my lecture. Join my discussion group. Join my church, synagogue, temple or Quaker Meeting. Subscribe to the Washington Post. Watch FOX news. Watch CNN. Follow the adult soaps on PBS.

Distrust the media? Get the news from social media. Listen to your family and friends. Take up a hobby. Chang jobs. Go into therapy. Get married. Stay single. Work out at the gym. Follow your dream. Find yourself. Be all you can be.

Follow your favorite teams on T.V. Make new friends. Drop old friends. Watch sports. Trust Google; worship the Cloud.

***

Sitting alone in the Sistine Chapel two hours before the chapel was open for visitors Bob Williams, also known as Pope Philip Neri, sat on the floor head down back against the wall sobbing.

***

It was a long meeting at *Beastly Bottoms*, Berne's best bistro. Surrounded by the mounted rear ends of bears, beavers, wild boars, African baboons and Australian bandicoots, purchased half off as leftovers from hunting lodges and Berne's little known *Multinational Mounted Mammals, Beastly Bottoms* is noted for its meaty menu. And for the secluded Small Mammals room in the back where Berne's elite leaders met to discuss common concerns and conflicts.

It was there ex-Madam President Hossenhoffer greeted her old friends Wiggy Schlossenmeir the friendly one, Hans Yodelgruber, the saucy one, and three newcomers from Berne's St. Peter and Paul, an independent Reformed Catholic cathedral. Senior Pastor Sophia, her husband deacon Lance Lott, dog master of the cathedral's world famous Dancing Dachshunds, who earned their keep by going on…

Woof!

The third member of the Peter and Paul party, Schatzi Schatzilee sired by Foodle and Brunie back on the windy cold Maine coast USA Schatzi was the spokesdog for the Dancing Dachshunds.

Miz Hossenhoffer began. "The news friends is not good. The pope has disappeared. His secretary, two nurses, and his chauffer, who facilitated his escape have refused to talk, pointing to the note pope Philip left. *Pray for me friends. Pray for the Church. Pray for the world. Pax Vovobiscum.*

Hans. "They've checked the monasteries?"

H & H (Hale and Hearty Hossenhoeffer) "Most have complied but a significant number, honoring his wishes, have refused to look for the pope,."

Hans. "But why would Philip disappear, leaving the Church without a leader in our global crisis? Schatzi! Damnit let go of my leg?"

Woof?

Hans. "You dogs could find the pope?"

"Woof, …… ….. .. ………. woof."

Hans. "What's she saying?"

Lance Lott. "They could but they won't?"

Hans. "Why the hell not, for God's sake?"

Woof…. ……….. ……. … ………. ……….. ……… *Woof.*

Hans. "What'd she say?"

Lance Lott. "She says let's do what the pope asked."

Hans. "Scheisse. For God's sake why?"

Woof….. ………. .. ……….. …….. *Woof.*

"Because she thinks the pope has no answer except to do what he asked us to do."

Wiggy. "So the Cloud of Unknowing can speak to us directly?"

Lance. "Yes."

***

A week later madam president, Hans and Wiggy, Pastor Sophia, deacon Lance Lott the canine impresario, and Schatzi the prize sausage hound were back in the Small Mammals room listening to Schatz's "Three Steps to the Cloud" proposal.

. . . first . . . ., ... is . . . .

Wiggy, "What was the last one?"

Lance translating.

"Sharing."

Wiggy. "And the first two again?"

"Cleansing and Waiting."

Knock Knock.

H. & H. "Yes?"

"We'll be closing in twenty minutes madam."

When Ms. Hoffenhoffer offered double overtime to *The Beastly Bottoms'* night manager and his staff it was agreed madam's small group might spend another hour in the Small Mammals room, decorated as you'd expect with rabbit rears, beaver butts, and…

Woof!

"Cleansing is sweeping away the unnecessary news we've all absorbed from Google and other unsavory sources. Waiting is turning around in Plato's dim and cluttered cave to breathe in the bright sky above and gaze into the Cloud of Unknowing."

Wiggy. "And Sharing?"

H & H. "Is sharing whatever comes out of the Cloud. Remember the monk and the buffalo?"

Hans. "No."

H & H. "A Buddhist monk was riding his buffalo up the mountain until the buffalo disappeared and the monk had to walk alone. As he reached the peak the monk disappeared. Then he rides the buffalo down the mountain and returns to his village."

Hans. "So what?"

H &H. "So the villagers learned to ride buffalos instead of killing them for food, and the crime rate dropped in half in the first six months."

Wiggy. "And the lesson for us is?"

"We're all monks climbing the mountain to get to the top."

Hans. "*The* mountain? Only one?"

H & H. "One mountain; many trails to the top. And then we return to the lonely crowd below, gathered in the village square quarreling and fighting under the warm rays of the unfiltered sun as the rising water inch by inch creeps across the barren land."

"Mountain or wasteland? Which is it?"

"Life is a mountain not a wasteland. It goes somewhere."

"Where?"

"Up."

Pause for reflection.

***

"Joyful, joyful we adore thee, God of glory God of..."

"Hello. This is abbot Joel at Daylesford abbey in Paoli Pennsylvania. How may..."

"Abbot Joel this is Hannah Hossenhoeffer from Berne."

"Good to hear your voice Hannah. What's up?"

"You got my e-mail?"

"On Philip's disappearance? Yes. What's your thought?"

"We follow the pope's advice. We contact the old crew; ask them to take a week off opening their hearts to the Cloud of Unknowing; on retreat or in reflection suited to their schedules. Then we share experiences, look for what God is saying to us, and see where we go from there."

"Sounds good to me. Who'd you like to contact?"

After dividing up the crew Joel shared abbey news, Hannah shared a bit of gossip on the upcoming Swiss presidential election; they wished each other well and hung up.

***

Joyful, joyful we adore You,
God of glory, God of love;
Hearts unfold like flowers before You
Opening to the sun above…
Giver of immortal gladness,
Fill us with the light of day….
Teach us how to love each other,
Lift us to the joy divine.

***

There are many ways to access the Cloud of Unknowing. Father Andrew and the Norbertines at Daylesford abbey had no problem. The cooks, cleaning ladies, and maintenance men were given a week's vacation with pay to spend time with their families and in prayer while the eighteen Fathers, and seven Sisters, covering for the staff, went on retreat spending time in prayer in their rooms, in secluded nooks throughout the abbey, or walking alone in God's great outdoors. Most fasted, a few did not.

In Berne Pastor Sophia, dog master Lance, and the dogs maintained silence until after lunch and then returned to the normal business of their busy lives: parish business and interchurch business for Sophia, rehearsals for the Christmas program for Lance and the dogs.

Professor Hank at Haverford took a week's leave of absence from teaching to go on retreat at Pendle Hill, a Quaker spiritual center outside Philadelphia founded in…

Woof.

Arnold Really O'Reilly, his wife Rita, Schatzi, Foodle, and Slim, Schatzi's older sibling, took long walks alone along the high ridge overlooking the shivering Atlantic.

But down south in Peachbush things were not going smoothly. Rabbi David Cohen, rebbetzina Ruth, and son Sam were fine, entering into *Atn Chonen*, the Jewish prayer for wisdom, "not by asking but in searching and wrestling." The Corries unfortunately had no idea what to do. The set prayers they'd learned in bible study didn't seem to fit, and the Yoga classes mizz Corrie enjoyed took her to a quiet place and left her there, stuck in neutral with the engine still running. Hossie tried fasting but he spent so much time fighting his lust for the goodies he soon forgot what he was there for. Finally Fred Corrie emailed Father Lopez at Our Lady of Guadalupe for help.

Sitting in the Corrie's living room with their cold Dr. Peppers and Dunkin Doughnuts Father Lopez asked each one what brought them closest to their peaceful place. Fred Corrie said "'When I'm playing golf on Saturdays with three old friends", Ruth Corrie mentioned her Yoga classes, and Hossie took a while to admit it was eating seven slices of mizz Cohen's kosher pizza and chocolate milk. Looking a bit flummoxed Father Lopez grinned sheepishly and said he'd have to get back to them.

Two days later the Corries read Father Lopez's email very carefully. Fred Corrie was to play nine holes of golf alone in the morning before the course got crowded. Mizz Corrie was to sit quietly for ten minutes after her Yoga class, go home and cook her favorite boiled peanuts soup in silence. Hossie was sit alone on the front porch eating a chocolate almond Hersey bar, repeating to himself "God (breath in) feeds (breath out) me (breath in)" over and over and over.

***

"Amazing."

"Hard to believe."

Zoomers madam ex-president Hossenhoeffer and abbot Joel starred at each other's glassy image miraculously transmitted across the dark Atlantic. Abbot Joel shrugged and shook his head; H & H laughed so hard she had to cover her mouth.

"Whoa."

"Whoa indeed."

"Not one objection. Not one."

"Even the dogs."

"Well at least we know what to do."

Pause.

"Honestly abbot what was your leading?"

"Same as everybody else's. What was yours?"

"Even the place. Here in Berne."

PART 2

AMAZING

CHAPTER 8

STORM CLOUDS AT NOON

"Good evening and welcome to Tucker Carlson, the most watched T.V. news show in America. My guest tonight is Henry Kissinger, who is still the smartest man in the room after decades shaping and defending American foreign policy in Vietnam, Argentina, Chile, and Pakistan."

Henry nods.

"Our friends on the left have criticized your political views as cynical and heartless. Some have called you a war criminal. How do you respond?"

"In the real world, as opposed to the liberals' wish world I repeat what I've said before. 'America has no permanent friends or enemies, only interests which must be defended by Power, the ultimate aphrodisiac.' Sometimes we win; sometimes, as in Vietnam, we lose, but the West's future depends on our ability to stem the tide of anti-American chaos."

"What are your views on Donald Trump?"

"When Trump came into office in 2016 I said he represented an extraordinary opportunity to advance American interests in foreign affairs. Today I still think that's true but I worry about his followers."

"What do you think of Alt-Right groups like the Oath Keepers, Proud Boys, and QAnon?"

"Their premature violence makes them dangerous distractions from my main concern; to preserve Western values in a world threatened on one side by Russian, Chinese, and Islamic anti-American civilizations, and on the other by the liberal's wish world, which abandons power for promises and piety."

"Thank you Mr. Secretary of State. This program will always welcome your perceptive take on the chaos we face. To end on a lighter note is there a thought sir you'd like to leave with us?"

"Corrupt politicians make the other 10% look bad."

"Thank you Henry if I may call you Henry. Back after this.... This is Tucker Carlson saying goodnight for the show that is the sworn enemy of lying, pomposity, smugness, and group think."

***

"I'll have the Rutti-Tutti-Fruity pancakes with sugar-free syrup and a cuppa coffee."

"Same for me. Cream and two sugars."

"Eggs, bacon, and toast."

"I'm sorry sir; that's not on the menu."

"But you do have bacon, eggs and toast?"

"Yes sir."

"Well that's what I'll have."

As Mildred Stanisloski, a blond middle-aged waitress with two children at home, in her light blue slightly soiled IHOP...

Woof.

Having ordered three hard-eyed men settled back in a lumpy black leather booth at the *International House of Pancakes* on Lancaster Ave. on the edge of the Haverford college campus.

Ex-president, ex-con, Dr. Sly Foxxy, Phd. in geology, opened the discussion. His old buddies in crime: Haverford college's men's soccer and tennis coach Coach Randalier, commonly known as Coach Randy for his one-on-one shower meetings with certain favored athletes, and Tim Rottenburger, a media major in his senior year, sitting across the table from the ex-president smiled for Foxxy to begin.

"I heard from Pastor Jones last week. He wants us involved in his Christmas Armageddon project."

Pause while Coach Randy and Tim waited.

"Three hundred apiece for you two."

Tim laughed. "You can't be serious. Even as an opening bid that's ridiculous."

"He says other expenses have limited his ability to..."

"Bullshit. He's got Texas oil barons and a Texas senior senator in his back pocket..."

Coach coughed to interrupt.

"What's our role?"

"He wants media major Tim, who has a daily half hour college T.V. news show, *Tim's Tidbits*, to interview me next Wednesday."

"And what will the celebrated Dr. Foxxy say?"

"I'll say I have a message in Latin, passed on to me for a price, by a lapsed Vatican cleaning lady, that the pope has ties to QAnon."

Tim snorted. "Whoa. Please. Nobody'll buy that."

"The notes are in the pope's handwriting, written on Vatican stationary. I'll also claim to have a recorded statement by the Archbishop of Canterbury to his fellow bishops directing them to encourage their parish priests to preach on the dire consequences of ignoring God's word on the coming Day of Judgement. Specifically on Christmas. In order to prepare for the great day. Anglicans, and American Episcopalians, are to be encouraged to join the ecumenical Armageddon for the Holidays movement."

"Please. Stop. I can't take any more." and Tim covered his face to muffle his suppressed hilarity and put his head down on the hard plastic tabletop, just as Mildred Stanisloski was bringing two Rutti-Tutti-Fruitti pancakes plus and Tim's Brit Bonanza: three eggs, four slices of crisp bacon, ham, fried potatoes, oatmeal, sausage, and a thin slice of to-ma-to.

***

Sequestered with the senator in Dewlittle's home office in Austin Pastor Jones sat comfortably in a plush Republican red swivel chair, with his pudgy fingers laced across his round middle aged middle waiting for the senator to begin the conversation on which much of his and the nation's future depended.

"What's your plan reverend?"

"I'm afraid I can't reveal our plans at this time senator."

"You do know I'm a very rich man reverend. That's why you contacted me."

"Yes sir, I know that but security…"

"Sir. Are you suggesting I'm a security risk?"

Pause.

Pause.

"I'm afraid sir this conversation is very close to being over."

"Senator can I get back to you?"

"Bullshit. I'm not a dummy, reverend. I checked. You don't need to check with anyone. You're it. The rest will do what they're told. So….. will you tell me what I'll be getting for my money for or won't you?"

Pastor Jones who'd feared it might come down to this closed his eyes, ruffled his shoulders, and settled into prayer. Three minutes later his eyes popped open.

"The Lord says you are to be trusted. The plan is to link the birth of Jesus on Christmas to the Second Coming. On Christmas Christ came to love and save the world. In the second coming Christ comes to judge the world. To separate sheep from goats. To separate those who accept Jesus Christ as their Lord and Savior from those who don't."

"Pastor Jones? May I speak freely?"

"Of course."

"Speaking for myself and the people I represent - not the voters for God's sake, but the influential set – we don't give a pheasant's fart who's saved and who's not. Our only goal is to fuck the Democrats in the next election. To keep the oil flowing from Texas, to privatize portions of our national parks to keep the economy humming, and protect our borders from…"

"I know your agenda Senator, and I believe we can work together. Your and your friend's contributions are a vital…"

"Pastor Jones?"

"Yes senator?"

"If Evangelicals opt out of the next election to wait on Armageddon…"

"We're lowballing Armageddon. The focus will be on the prophetically proclaimed Day of Judgement."

"Whatever you call it Pastor if your people are waiting to be wafted away into heaven they sure as hell aren't going to vote in this world."

"The plan is to paint the ungodly liberals as demonic agents of Satan, who must be defeated to prepare the way for God's glorious Judgement Day. Most of my people believe that already."

Raising his glass of fifteen year old Pappy Van Winkle bourbon the senior senator from Texas smiled across at Pastor Jones, who nodded, and the deal was sealed.

***

"The bloodhound bleeds."

"'The horsefly nips the tiger's tail."

"Everything in place?"

"Christmas eve."

"We're fuckin' ready."

"Keep the faith."

CHAPTER 9

SUNSHINE AT MIDNIGHT

If *Ephesians 4: 6 "God... is over all through all and in all"* is true then all we need to do is open our eyes and God is there, open our ears and God is there, and open our hearts and God is there. Thank you Lord for all the people who are in my heart."

***

Alone with her guests in the Small Mammals room at the bustling bistro Beastly Bottoms Swiss ex-madam president's ruddy Yorkshire face was beaming. Then, putting down her brimming glass of Guinness on the hard glass table, she asked where the others were. Hannah H & H had good news to share and she was impatient to have everyone present. Wiggy shrugged but Pastor Sophia from St. Peter and Paul's reformed Catholic cathedral said she'd seen Hans and dog master Lance Lott outside talking.

"They'll be in a minute... Where's Schatzi?"

"Under the table curled around my feet. She's thinking of the hundred and fifty dogs back in the cathedral napping on caramel-colored cedar benches in the nave under..."

Woof. Woof.

"Under the watchful eye of Mary" madam ex-president went on, "the saints, and Jesus who's been a dog lover since the beginning."

"What?"

"Dogs were the first psychotherapists. When the cave people had their inevitable disagreements it was dogs; big, little, furry and smooth skinned who wandered aimlessly from one angry voice to another begging for attention. Attention that redirected angry energy into more thoughtful ways of resolving their differences. Great Danes and prehistoric poodles…"

"Ahem. Hack. Cough. Cough."

Startled by the interruption Hannah refocused on the topic at hand.

"Wiggy and I have not heard one objection. Not one. A third had no response either way but the rest all said the same thing in different ways. Come together in small groups and let the Spirit take it from there. Arnold in Maine was romping with Slim, Schatzi's stay at home older sibling, on the lawn overlooking the wide Atlantic when he heard the words 'Come together. Dogs and people. One big yappy family.' What are you hearing Pastor Sophia?"

"Ich bin fassungslos. I can't believe it. Amazing. A few no comment comments, but everyone else in Atlantic City heard the Cloud saying "Come together in small groups."

"What did the dogs hear Wiggy?"

"Lance said they got two messages. One: "stay close to the food", and two "Your owners need you."

"Any thoughts on what's next?... Pastor Sophia?"

"Contact our friends in Rome and the States. If the Cloud spoke clearly to us we must assume the Cloud spoke clearly to the others."

"Wiggy you have a thought?"

"No. I was just stretching."

Pause.

"Finally. There you are. We were just getting started."

"Sorry we're late."

"Was it important?"

"We think so. Hans and I would like to research Cloud-centered communities in history. What Dr. King called the Beloved Community. Hans from the beginning up until the first Franciscans."

"And Lance from then on."

Arf. Woof. Arf aft aft.

"What is it Schatzile?"

Woof..... .... ?

"Schatzi says she needs an outdoor break."

And so it was agreed madam president would contact absent friends and Hans and Lance would look into the past. While Lance led Schatzi out Hans raised his hand half way for attention.

Pause.

"Before we break up I have a concern."

"Yes Hans."

"Are we allowed to use our brains to discuss our progress, or must we depend on a mystical union with the Cloud over every minor decision that comes along?"

That discussion went on for forty minutes until it was decided we'd been given our brains to implement what Quakers call Openings to seek fresh guidance from above. Or within. Or wherever. When Hans asked who decides what's essential and what's not, sensing that discussion might go on unresolved for some time, madam ex-president suggested the group wait for responses from Rome and the States before considering the next step; which didn't answer Hans' question but would allow the little group to use the facilities and move on.

Hans smiled thinking to himself that fifty-fifty wasn't bad, everyone chipped in to pay the bill, and the little group left by the secret passage that led to the waiting beer truck that would disperse Hannah's helpers unobserved back to their homes.

Meanwhile curious customers sitting in the main dining area were wondering why madam president's little group had been in the Small Mammals room for over two hours. Ex-Haverford president Dr. Foxxy, secluded in the corner sipping schnapps and nibbling on a stale apple strudel however had a pretty good idea what was going on behind the green door.

***

"All in?"

Two days later reunited behind the forest green door in the Small Mammals room Hannah Hossenhoeffer looked at her little group for a response. Hans answered "Yo"; the rest nodded.

"Wiggy?"

"The Peachbush bunch are fine. Same as us. Amazing. Hossie got the strongest response."

> *Forget Pastor Jones and Armageddon, forget the Proud Boys, and Foxxy's crafty coterie at Haverford. Live into the future day by day with the sisters and brothers around you. Follow the Cloud. Leave madam president's group in Berne to communicate with Cloud minded mystics around the world."*[6]

"Danke schon Wiggy. Sophie?"

"I talked with Dorothy Day number 3 at St. Mike's in Atlantic City."

"Where?"

"New Jersey."

"What's number three?"

"Strange story. About five years ago four young women in their twenties working in the East Side slums in New York met Dorothy Day. Independently they each felt a calling to take vows; first as a Catholic and later as a Franciscan Sister of the Renewal in Camden. Each young woman felt drawn to the name Sister Dorothy Day. Their Mother Superior, Teresa of Avila, pondered the dilemma and decided the four Sisters had been called as a group to serve God among the poor and that each one was entitled to the name they'd been given in prayer. Hence Sisters Dorothy Day Two, Three, Four, Five."

"And one?"

"Jesus of course."

"That's spooky."

[6] Written notices like scripture, songs, and poems are italicized. As are a character's unspoken thoughts.

"The whole things spooky. The Ten Commandments are spooky, the Resurrection's spooky. There are spooky bits woven all through Christianity's tattered tapestry. Golden threads among the..."

Woof, arf, woof.

"Lance?"

"Abbot Joel was away but I talked with Father Andrew. The ex-pickpocket from Atlantic City. He said he'd had his revelation on the boardwalk across from the old Steele Pier. What he heard was 'Renew the Norbertines'. Starting with the Norbertines at Daylesford abbey."

"Go on."

"He said he'd share his Leading, as Quakers call it, with abbot Joel when he returned."

"Hans?"

"Not so good."

"Go on."

"We never really got to the Cloud. Professor Hank is a most interesting guy. We talked about post-modern metaphysics: Heidegger and Alain Badiou. The difference there is between Heidegger's...."

"Hans."

"I know. Stick to the Cloud."

Seeing everyone had finished their snapps and strudel Hannah asked if anyone had a last thought. Sophie, who'd been doing yoga twice a week nodded and began.

Breath at the pace of the slow sun's rising
Grow in grace to the season's curve
Ride the crest of rolling creation
Make friends with time.[7]

***

Later.

Seated comfortably outdoors at the Tingle-Kringle café, sharing a light late lunch of cheese fondu laced with cherry brandy, and Kaffee-crème for some and Roussette from Savoy, a cut above most dry French wines,

---

[7] /Author's poem.

the Berne bunch waited patiently for Hannah to move the conversation beyond friendly small talk into wider concerns.

"Hans. How goes the research into Dr. King's Beloved Communities?"

"To start with the groups were small and go way back. Noah and his household found favor with God to escape the sinner-soaked Flood. Moses and the prophets had faithful supporters but not many. Christ's contemporary followers lived together after his death for forty years in Jerusalem…"

Woof.

"What?"

Woof?...... .... Woof?"

"Shatzi says slow down, she's having a hard time following."

"I'll try but you can always catch her up later Lance. Now where was I?.... After Christ died his followers continued to worship in the Temple, sharing all things in common. Paul established Beloved Communities at most of the major cities scattered around Mare Nostrum, Our (Roman) Sea."

"And later?"

"The first Franciscans, Francis, Clare and their followers lived in joyous devotion to Lady Poverty. It's quite likely Francis and his lay brothers were also pre-Pentecostals; praising God in prayer, song, and heavenly tongues during their inspired devotions in the mountains around Assisi. Certainly Francis was on intimate terms with Brother Sun and Sister Moon, Mother Earth and Sister Bodily Death."

When Hans finished there were no response and the little group settled into silence.

And from silence into stillness.

And from stillness into the shared fellowship of the Beloved Community.

CHAPTER 10

THE LONG LOOK THAT LINGERS

Meanwhile back in the Peach State plans for the Second Coming of Christ on Christmas were proceeding apace. Drawing together a diverse coalition of interests with only two weeks left Pastor Jones was sharing his satisfactions and concerns with his old friend deacon Billy Bob Bestbuddy in the Pastor's office behind the sanctuary.

"Another Jack Daniels?"

"Just a touch."

"Been a long journey Billy. The aborted Easter attempt three years ago. We were so close in Rome."

He sighed and grimaced regret.

"How's James J?"

"We may never know. You know he left the church after the pope intervened for his release. No one's heard from him since. I... my own flesh and blood."

"Weren't your fault Jim."

"I know but it's hard. I'll never know if he missed the pope on purpose or if his arm were jostled at the critical moment. In any case he missed, and Armageddon was delayed."

"Till now Jim."

"Right." And the reverend's eyes narrowed and his face tightened into the long look that lingered Billy Bob had seen before."

"Only two weeks left till Christmas. You ready?"

"As ready as we can be."

"Jim can I ask you a question?"

"Yes?"

"Why are we working with thugs like the Proud Boys? And that shifty ex-con, Dr. Foxxy and his buddies up North? If Armageddon's a spiritual event why can't we depend on our people; not certified sinners?"

"You want the Lord works in mysterious ways answer or a more practical response?"

"Just the second."

"Since the disaster in Rome on Easter a coupla years ago, most of our lot are leery of hearing me, or anybody else, preach on the Second Coming, Judgement Day, or Armageddon."

"So why do it?"

"Because, Billy Bob, I hear the same voice inside telling me to trust the Lord and never give up. Same as before."

Not for the first time deacon Bestbuddy gave his pastor and boyhood friend a long look. It weren't Jim's views, or even his mission, that was unsettling. It was the look in Jim's eyes. As if Jim were no longer there. Billy Bob sensed he was looking at something or someone who was mocking him. Someone whose eyes were lit with a fierce insanity that shrieked for expression.

He'd seen that look before but always Billy Bob's love and humor and a bit more Jack Daniels than they'd planned on had brightened the dark light in Jim's eyes. This time was different.

"Jim baby" he whispered "don't go there. Please."

"I don't know what you're talking about Billy. I'm fine. I feel better than I have in weeks... You want another shot before you go? I know you don't have to get up early tomorrow."

After their brief parting Billy Bob went to spend a few minutes in the sanctuary, while Jim smiled and whispered to himself, *"I'm glad that's over."*

CHAPTER 11

THREE DAYS BEFORE CHRISTMAS

I

"Thank you for allowing the United Sates to be reborn. We love you and thank you. In Christ's holy name we pray."

"Play it again Sara."

And so Sara Snoop, ace anchorwoman at PBS, rewound the tape and the small group in the PBS newsroom listened for the third time to QAnon's present leader, Jake Angeli's (born Jacob Chansley), prayer at president Trump's January 2021 insurrection.

Dressed in shamanic attire: buffalo horned headgear, tri-colored painted face, Norse gods and neo-Nazi symbols tattooed to his bare chest and arms, low slung satyr like chinos carrying an eight foot spear in one hand and an American flag in the other Jake Angeli was a – the? - living icon for the far right. Especially for one third of Republicans who support QAnon's core belief that Democrats and liberals around the world are satanic baby eating pedophiles who are masterminding worldwide child sex trafficking.

"That'll work."

"Where Ken?"

"Just after the Pizzagate bit."

"Long or short?"

"Just a passing reference. Shortly before Trump's 2016 victory Twitter and other social media reported the FBI had raided a pizzeria in the nation's capital suspected of harboring a satanic ring of pedophiles. In the 2020 presidential election cycle the story resurfaced on Tik Tok where it was seen by 80 million viewers."

"The Hilary lead-in that..."

"Won't be needed. We have the Trumpsters take on Hilary in several other bits. Any other comments? Good. We'll break for lunch and resume at two. John can I see you for a moment?"

"Certainly Mr. Burns."

***

A week before Christmas Pastor Jones was on the phone with senior senator Darlington Dewlittle from Texas asking for money again. Lots of money.

"Pastor?"

"Yes senator?"

"Three times what we agreed on? What the hell's going on?"

"Big news senator."

"It's always big news. What is it this time?"

"Armageddon starts on Christmas."

"Easter didn't work out; now it's Christmas? How 'bout Halloween?"

"I'm serious."

"Shit pastor you're always serious. I've got a called election coming up in January. Time is money. Tell me. What's the plan this time and how does it get me reelected?"

"Can't tell you the plan, senator, except that it begins on Christmas."

Pause.

"Pastor, you must know my backers aren't going to put up hard cash without any idea what it's going for. You and I both know this is good ole' Texas bullshit. Look I gotta go. Don't call again."

Click.

Twenty minutes later the senior senator from the Lone Star state got a text message suggesting if they didn't talk again Pastor Jones would be forced to share possibly incendiary information about the senator's personal life.

Ten minutes later Pastor Jones got a text that Mr. and Mrs. Harvey Smith's sign-in signature at the Shining Moment motel just outside Peachbush, Georgia was the same as Pastor Jones'.

***

You're a grand old flag, and forever in peace may you wave. You're the emblem of the land I love, the home of the free and the brave.

You have reached the answering service of senior senator Darlington Dewlittle from the great state of Texas. Please leave...."

"Senator Dewlittle?"

"I thought you might be calling Jim. What's on your mind?"

"I'll risk it. You leak your unfounded rumor and I'll leak mine. If I go down it won't matter. After the first Armageddon fiasco my name's mud anyway. . If you go down no member of the Dewlittle family ..."

Woof.

Not one to chase runaway rabbits senator Dewlittler returned to square one.

"Pastor, you win. What's the plan and how does it help me get reelected in purple-poised Texas?"

"All I know is it starts on Christmas."

"Who does know?"

"The Proud Boys."

"Son are you nuts? The Proud Boys! What do they care about Armageddon? They're into killing national notables to create chaos and bring down the government. Hell Jim I'm the government. I'd be out of a job."

"Chaos is the point. Think about it. What happens when our noble citizens are threatened with chaos? They turn to the righteous right. Nixon, George W. and The Donald. Chaos is no time to discuss the issues. Martial law under Trump, you're reelected in a landslide and the commie liberal media, spearheaded by CNN and the New York Times are banned as un-American subversive organizations. Besides senator you really have no choice have you?"

***

Meanwhile ex-college president, ex-con, Dr. Sly Foxxy hearing rumors of discussions between Pastor Jones and the senior senator from Texas was feeling shut out. Unable to reestablish himself in the academic world and low on funds Fred hired an investigative reporter to dig up dirt on Pastor Jones and senator Dewlittle from Texas.

What the private eye found was pretty much what Pastor Jones and senator Dewlittle each knew about the other.

***

You're a grand old flag, and forever in peace may you wave. You're the emblem of the land I love, the home of the free and the brave. You're a…

"Senator?"

"This is senator Dewlittle from the great state of Texas. Yes Dr. Foxxy?"

"I thought you'd return my call. How much can I put you down for?"

"Nothing. You can put me down for nothing."

"Now senator let's not waste time. We both know I can ruin your career, and Pastor Jones' too if that's any consolation."

"It's your word, the work of an ex-con, against a United States senator."

"Except this ex-con has the paperwork for Darlington Dewlittle's arrest and conviction for dealing drugs as a teenager at family gatherings. Advertised as pep pills left over from a school science fair Darlington was…

Woof. Woof. Woof.

"Plus…"

"Plus what?"

"Plus this conversation has been recorded for quality purposes."

Click.

***

I wish I was in Dixie. Hooray! Hooray!

In Dixie land I'll take my stand

To live and die in Dixie.

Away, away, away down South in Dixie.

"Greeting you'all. You've reached the Lily White Church in the Valley in Peachbush Georgia. We're sorry we're unable to take your call at this time. If you'll leave a call-back number with a brief message someone from

Pastor Jones's team of dedicated downhome Christians will return your call as soon as possible."

"Please tell Pastor Jones Haverford college ex-president, Dr. Foxxy called concerning an unpaid bill from the Shining Moment motel. He has my number."

***

You're a grand old flag, and forever in peace may you wave. You're the emblem of the land I love, the home of the free and the brave.

..."Yes, yes I know who you are. What I don't know is why the Proud Boys can't tell us about Operation Chaos. I thought we were working together to throw the commie bastards out."

"I'm sorry senator. You know as much as we do."

*But....... ....***####...... ....!*

"Yes I realize your re-election depends entirely on the Proud Boys. So do our Christmas plans."

.... ?

"I tried. They said they have all the money they need. Tarrio said they don't trust us with any information which might leak to the media."

****&&&.....#####.......&&###.... .... &&###%%*!!*

"Senator I don't care how pissed off you are. The Proud Boys don't need our money and I don't know of a snitch we could buy off. So frankly senator get over it. Tarrio assured me the Storm would...

"..........&&&%%%##. ....?"

"It's a QAnon term. First there's the Great Awakening when the public wakes up to Satan at work behind the liberal establishment; then there's the Storm when action is taken to ferret out the Deep State and eliminate ***%%%%### liberals."

Pause.

"......... ... . Trump ....!"

"Good idea senator. Let me know how that goes. Look I've got a meeting. Love to Mary and the kids."

Click.

***

I wish I was in Dixie. Hooray! Hooray!
In Dixie land I'll take my stand
To live and die in…

"This is Pastor Jones. Good to hear your voice senator. He did? That sounds promising. You're sure?"

"……… ……... …. ?"

"Speak up senator. We have a bad connection."

"Trump said he's going on all channels at 8: 00 tonight. He didn't say what he'd say. He probable doesn't know himself."

"What's your best guess senator?"

"That B.A.R., the Black Armed Revolution, a previously unidentified Trumped up domestic terror organization, plans to invade the White House on Christmas Eve. Their war cry is "I'm Dreaming of a Black Christmas." Loyal citizens are advised to stay indoors and let local law enforcement and the military deal with the bastards."

"Bastards?"

"I wouldn't be surprised."

Pause.

"Where's that leave us Jim?"

Pause.

"Big question senator. Why don't we check with our people and I'll call you back."

"You check with the Bible Belt top brass and I'll sound out the good ole boys here in Washington. After Trump's speech, we'll get their input, and I'll give you a call tomorrow early afternoon. Only three days left till Christmas. Take care."

"Bless you senator and the Lord's work you're doing."

Click.

***

"Jim?"

"I'm here but there's nothing to talk about. The speech was over the top even for Trump. The senators I talked with are saying to lay low. Give it a few days before we get involved. Whatta your folks saying?"

"First you were right on. Even the reference to Black Christmas. Most have called for a national day of prayer. Can't hurt. Armageddon may be right on the brink; then again who knows what'll happen. I'm with you. Stay low for a week or so. We'll be in touch. Love to Mary."

***

"Good evening. Thank you for joining the PBS News Hour. Our lead story is that after president Trump's hair-raising rant the marines have been called in to help protect the White House. B.L.M. and every Black protest groups across the board deny any involvement and claim Trump is trying to start a race war. The American Association of Psychologists in an unusually blunt public statement say Trump is "off his rocker." Republicans are staying indoors glued to FOX news. Moderate Democrats are also indoors glued to CNN while progressive Democrats are peacefully gathering to confront the armed Trumpsters who've joined the marines in defense of the White House and their beloved president."

"Arnold?"

"Yes."

"It's Jack from the Proud Boys. We got a problem."

"Yes?"

"Tarrio got wind I been talking outside the Boys. He don't know who, but…

"Where are you Jack?"

"White Plains outside New York."

"Have you money?"

Laughter.

"I cleaned out the emergency fund fore I left."

"Take a train…"

Laughter.

"I can hire a helicopter, a private jet."

"Traceable."

"A limo?"

"Under another name. Drive to Bar Harbor Maine. Call 40" before you get there and I'll meet you at the Barnacle Restaurant downtown. I'll take it from there."

"Arnold?"

"Yes?"

"I gotta a few questions."

"Save em till you get here."

"But I need to know..."

"Not now. You're too hot to know things you don't need to know."

"You better be on the level."

"I'm the best option you got Jack. Truly this could be a big break for both of us. And the future of our country. Stay well buddy. See you in Bar Harbor."

Click.

***

"Gentle reader."

"Yes."

"You still with us?"

"Barely, but why ask me? I'm only one. You need a wider sample."

"Right now it's a tie. You're the last one. Your opinion is critical. Half are carried along because they're curious or interested in bits of the narrative. Or they identify with Hannah and the stout lads in Berne or Hossie and Sam in Peachbush or...

WOOF WOOF ARF!!

"Or the dogs."

"And the other half?"

"Have dropped out. Too complicated. Story wise and philosophy wise. Story wise it's damn near impossible to follow the snarly narrative threads: Berne, Haverford, Daylesford abbey, Peachbush Georgia, Texas, Maine, Boise Idaho, and there must be more.

Philosophy wise you've lost the tension between the two clouds. I can't even remember what they are."

"The Cloud of Knowing and the Cloud of Unknowing. Human knowledge and opinion versus God's wisdom. Maybe you need to read it again to get the full..."

"Why would I read it again if I didn't like the first reading?"

Pause.

"So. I can put you down as interested but undecided. Thanks so much for your input gentle reader."

"I'm not your gentle reader. I'm a no. A definite no. You can take your book and..."

WOOF...... .... ! Woof.

"Well of course you'd object. You and your dogs are part of the problem, but since I was asked put me down as a definite no."

Click.

***

Hannah and the stout lads, Hans and Wiggy, sitting comfortably in slick black leather swivel chairs in the back room at Beastly Bottoms were glued to their computers, well not actually glued but attentive to the voices and images of Abbot Joel and Father Andrew Zooming from America.

Abbot Joel had just finished his weekly update on the Beloved Communities in the US. Sister Dorothy Day Three' best seller Lost in the Cloud had attracted forty or so fed up with it all, young and old, who'd been led to join the staff at St. Mike's as a third order Franciscan community. Hossie and his family in Peachbush had joined Father Lopez's Our Lady of Guadeloupe, the church across the tracks, and were sharing all things in common. The Corries were learning Spanish, momma Corrie and Fred were teaching classes in Living Southern, and Hossie a running back on the Burly Bears, the local high school football team, had carried the team to the state quarter finals.

Rabbi Cohen's congregation had bought a fifty five acre pecan farm, renovated the old farmhouse, created several two story motel style buildings, and was attending the local community college to learn the art of raising pecans. Their innovative kibbutz, Nuts to You, was attracting wide attention in the national Jewish community.

"Any comments?... Hans?"

"Last I heard Arnold was meeting Jack the renegade Proud Boy with a conscience in Bar Harbor. Hopefully Jack can tell us the Proud Boys' plans to disrupt Christmas. Let's take a break while I call Arnold."

Pause.

"Arnold? It's Hannah. Is Jack there?"

"... .. ... . but .... talk ... . It's .... EU time."

"Sorry. I'll call back in the morning. About 9: 00 your time..... Auf Wiederschn."

".... .. ."

***

"Arnold? This is Hannah again in Berne. Can we do this on Zoom? Readers are having trouble understanding your… Fine I'll send you the link….Ah there you are. You look great."

"Sea air and lobster roll."

"For breakfast?"

"For lunch. Lobster Newburgh on toast with white wine for dinner. How are things in Berne?"

"The Spirit's moving among us Arnie. Seriously. I can't believe how the Beloved Community is taking hold among the Norbertines at Dayleford, the Corrie's and Cohen's in Georgia, St. Mike's in AC..."

"Well the news here isn't so good. Jack who's careful to remain off screen says the Proud Boys have linked up with the Oath Keepers, QAnon and other homegrown terrorists to raise hell on Christmas but he doesn't know how. The original plan was to dynamite the Capitol but plans changed when Jack left knowing the specifics of plan one. We do know the Proud Boys contacted Trump who's lending his support behind the scenes. The good news is Blessed Communities are popping up everywhere."

Pause.

"It's good to see you Hannah. You still look hail and hearty. Any questions? Wiggy?... Hans? You always have a perceptive comment?"

"What should we do next?"

"Pray for guidance."

"Hans? Is that you? You think; you don't pray."

"I'm stuck Arnold. I don't know what we should do. Stay faithful to the Cloud of Unknowing in our little communities so there's something to build on after the chaos? Or take up arms against a sea of troubles?"

"We'll keep that in mind Hans. Good to see your face again, but you could use a shave. Ciao."

CHAPTER 12

CHRISTMAS EVE CHAOS

"Is this a great country or what? Greatest country on earth. Some say I'm the greatest president since Lincoln but that's not for me to say. Two terms? They said I was done. Hey Biden, hey Hilary, who's done now? But no hard feelings. Joe you needed a vacation… at your age. Hilary. How's prison life going? I hear you're writing a book. Be sure to spell my name right. But seriously my fellow Americans I'm not here to bring up old issues. It's Christmas eve for Crist's sake. Like that? Bit edgy but right on, for we are celebrating the holiday for Christ sake. But let's move on. I'm here to make a monumental announcement tonight. Huge! One that will change the course of history. One that will…"

Bang!

***

I wish I was in Dixie. Hooray Hoo…

"Jim. What the hell's going on? Trump's dead. Twenty three Senators home for the holidays, Democrats and Republicans, killed or wounded. Looting, killings, the Capitol's on fire. State capitols are burning. T.V. black out in half the country. Dams blown up. Flooding. What the hell's going on Jim?"

"Armageddon baby. It's God's time now. It's here at last. Thank God Almighty it's here at last?"

"I thought we were in this together. I thought we were working together to bring down the government, not the whole country."

"You had your chance senator."

"Shit. Holy shit. I've an election coming up in January."

"You *had* an election coming up."

"Jesus Ch..."

"I wouldn't say that Jim. Jesus is closer than you think."

"Have you seen him yet?"

"He's comin'. He'll be here."

"You know what I see Jim? Fires and floods and dead people. Chaos and no Christ.... O dear God. My poor people, and all because Proud Boys, QAnon, and people like you are nuts. Especially QAnon...."

"Jim?"

Silence.

"Pastor Jones?

Silence.

"This thing's not over. I'm sorry you misunderstood my intentions, but it's not over. Keep the line open. We may still need each other. Our followers are in shock now, but as time moves on, they may need a steady hand at the wheel. You and I need to be ready to be that steady hand."

"You're not sure are you?"

"Course I'm sure. Keep the lines open senator. God bless. May the Lord of Heaven..."

Click.

Sitting in his air-conditioned corner suite in downtown Houston senator Dewlittle looked over at his private secretary who was on the other line.

"So. What do you think?"

"I think he's not sure."

"Me too. Get me the list of our big donors. And a double expresso with two chocolate cream doughnuts."

***

Aus dem grauen Luftgebilde
Brocht die Sonne klar und mildedei
Und die fromme Seele ahnt.
Gott im hehren Vaterland.

"Hannah? This is Joel from America. I'm here with the Norbertine Crisis Council: Fathers Andrew, Hubert, and Sister Phyllis Martin."

….. …….. ……. …. ?

'Hubert's our resident artist and a spiritual director. He wears 1960's flair pants with the fly buttons on the outside. You know Andrew; and Sister Phyllis. She was one of Joe Biden's private secretaries for ten years before she got the call to be a Norbertine.

You asked for our input on the chaos in the States. Nothing definite. Keep the faith; build up the Beloved Communities in America, stay tuned. And you?"

"Europe's dealing with its own chaos. Most people are staying off the streets at home. Wide spread looting, well-traveled bridges and expressways blown up, Sweden's water has been poisoned. The Vatican's been sacked. Twice. In Hungry and Romania dead victims of the Delta virus are piled up and cremated in parking lots outside overcrowded hospitals.

Most here are terrified. Every effort to restore order has been countered by far right nationalist and neo-Nazi hate groups. The veneer of civilization, which had held humanity's dark impulses in check has been flipped over like a rotting tree lying helpless on the ground exposed to maggots, giant beetles and centipedes, poisonous flying insects all feeding on what was once a strong and growing tree. It's as if Goya's and Bosch's nightmares have fled from the Unconscious to materialize in our ordinary everyday world."

Silence. Sadness. Sorrow. Until Sister Phyllis asked about news from the Cloud.

Hannah sighed.

"Same as yours. Keep the faith; build up the Beloved Community, and wait."

"Well at least we're hearing the same word on both sides of the Atlantic. Anyone have anything to say before we close?"

"I'd like an English translation of your Swiss-German cell phone greeting."

"It's from the Swiss national hymn.
"Pierce the gloom in which we cower
with thy sunshine's cleansing power.
Then we'll feel and understand
that God dwelleth in this land ."
Click.

***

Hank our Quaker theologian reflects on the social implications of chaos, with occasional comments from the class.

"A widespread social calamity, like the chaos alluded to above, elicits a variety of responses, depending on the nature of the various groups being affected. Yes Pamela?"

"Will this lecture..."

"Be on the midterm? Perhaps, but don't take notes, just listen and when I'm done write two or three sentences that summarizes your response to what you've heard."

"Thank you sir."

"Arms dealers and others supplying the money-making materials needed to wage war are pleased. Warriors, on both sides, must deal with death, fear of and hatred for the enemy and loyalty for one's brothers and sisters in arms. Civilians must cope with loving anxiety for the beloved warriors far from home. Politicians and generals must balance public bravado with victory oriented in-house strategy. Medical personnel grieve the pain and dying of an unending stream of mutilated human bodies. The religious folks in and out of the military must factor in their understanding of God's will in the ongoing carnage.

Pastor Jones and those sympathetic to his views, see chaos in a positive light as Armageddon; God's war against Satan's liberal armies on earth. Secular minded alt-right Trumpsters are also encouraged by chaos which presents an opportunity to take back America from foreign invaders from shithole black, countries and their commie friends in Congress. And from the lingering influence of Hilary and..."

Ring! Ring! "You have reached..."

"Sorry professor. I forgot to turn it off."

"Next time forget to bring it to class."

Pause.

"Money makers like our own ex-president, ex-con, Sly Foxxy and president Eisenhower's military-industrial complex are focused on turning chaos into cash."

"And the Deep State?"

"A catch-all term for the Satan worshipping pedophiles who run the government, the economy, and the media. A useful term we may come back to later."

"And..."

"The good guys? The Beloved Communities we discussed last week each have their own areas of interest but are driven by their common allegiance to the Cloud of Unknowing. In short most suffer from war, some benefit, some grieve for lost loved ones; some are healers, and some are peacemakers."

***

Meanwhile in a secluded hut on the slopes of Popocatepetl "Smoking Mountain" the second highest and most active volcano in Mexico, Bob Williams, a retired catholic priest, is being cared for by the Lopez family of four who are impressed by their guest's educated Spanish and quiet manner. The money's good, not extravagant but good, and Roberto's easy to care for. During the working day he often accompanies Manuel and his two sons looking for lost climbers and helping the family raise corn, beans and coffee. It had been agreed at the final meeting with the local bishop that Father Williams was to be left to his prayers three hours a day, one hour of which was devoted to pondering an old art book on the Sistine Chapel.

Meditating on the separation between Noah's blessed community safe on the ark, and the sinners left behind on shore or quarreling in a small boat trying to catch up with the rest of their lives on the ark, Bob is drawn to the sinners. A toddler clinging to his mother's leg as she holds a weeping babe close in her arms. A man carrying his terrified wife on his back to what they hope will be safety; and a young woman, her husband, their toddler, and a burro clustered together, make it clear where Michelangelo's sympathies lay.

Later that afternoon Father Williams, at the daily mass with the Lopezs and several other mountain families, announces he'll be returning to his old home up north.

CHAPTER 13

THE LONESOME VALLEY

Pastor Jones' in person meeting in his office behind the sanctuary in Peachbush did not start well. The senator from the great state of Texas was furious the Proud Boys had shot Trump.

"You killed the movement Enrique. Trump was our leader. Our Moses. Jesus Christ what were you thinking?"

"He wasn't *our* fuckin' leader. Not after January 6th. Not after he deserted the insurrection he'd started. For us it was never about getting Trump a second term. Fuckin' politician."

"What the hell are you after?"

"Throw the bastards out. Start over. America for real Americans."

"And who's going to run this new America?"

"We'll figure that out after we get rid of the trash, but they'll be patriots, like us."

"Like it was in the beginning? Killing Indians? And slavery?"

"Why not? Fuckin' government's been coddling darkies and spics long enough. Now it's our turn."

Pause.

Pause.

"Enrique?"

"Yes."

"It's not about overturning the government is it?"

"Not really."

"It's about riots and killing?"

Silence.

"Look I gotta go. Lemme know how your little talk goes."

Tarrio leaves.

Pause.

"Whiskey anyone?"

Darlington and Foxxy nod. The QAnon lone stranger wearing an Armageddon Now mask shakes his head no.

Refueled after fifteen minutes the big three get down to business. Q argues for framing the chaos as the early days of Armageddon; Senator Dewlittle pushes for his being re-elected to keep Republicans in power in order to undermine the non-executive branches of government clearing the way for an unnamed prominent public figure, preferably from a western state, as America's first PFL, president for life.

Ex-college president Dr. Foxxy doesn't care how things go as long as he gets his cut. Stuck in swampy silence with no answers Q finally speaks.

"What about this? We know the Proud Boys and Oath Keepers will raise more hell. Right?"

"Right.

"So?"

"So reluctantly president Pence is forced by public opinion to declare martial law. The Proud Boys create more chaos and an exhausted and terrified citizenry are re-energized to join QAnon's war between good and evil."

"And then?"

"Won't matter. If QAnon's right we're all in Gods' hands. If we aren't right we go back to America for Americans with a new Moses in charge. In either case the liberal cabal is driven from power. It's win win."

"And my cut?"

"If there is no God Dewlittle will appoint you Secretary of Treasury. If there is a God you'll probably go to hell."

"I won't go alone."

***

Joyful joyful we adore thee.
God of glory, God of love,
Hearts unfold....
"Joel?"
"Bob."
"Can we meet in Rome? Bring Hannah and Joel. No more than six. Just inside the door by the Pieta. Day after tomorrow 10: 00."

***

Jesus walked this lonesome valley.
He had to walk it by himself.
Nobody else could walk it for him.
He had to walk it by himself.
You must walk this lonesome valley.
You have to walk it by yourself.
Nobody else can walk it for you.
You have to walk it by yourself.

Five days out from Christmas a hooded Franciscan tour guide waved his "Go Lobos" elevated flag to gather his little group of tourists together to admire Michelangelo's Madonna and child just inside St. Peters. Then leading the little group through the vast wonders of the pope's church to a large room not open to the public behind the huge canopied altar, the tour guide shut the door and removed his cowl.

Abbot Joel was the first to respond to the pope's open arms.

"Bob! God it's good to see you." Then stepping back Joel took a long look at his old friend.

"You look well. You could use a shave but you look well Your Holiness. Really well."

Then Joel stepped aside to allow the others to greet Pope Philip. As each of the tourists stepped forward for a papal embrace the pope had words of appreciation mixed with a few tears for all they'd suffered in the past year.

It was a small group: Norbertines: Sister Phyllis Martin and Father Andrew with the abbot; Swiss president in waiting[8] Hale and Hearty Hannah Hossenhoeffer and two of her stout lads, Wiggy and Hans.

As they gathered in a circle the pope said a short prayer and asked for input from each tourist. When five minutes passed and no one had responded they fell into the shared silence permeated by the blessed Clod. After thirty minutes pope Philip opened his eyes, smiled, and began.

"You all know the reason I left Rome was to seek God' will in the Cloud of Unknowing. I returned because the inner word I'd been seeking spoke to me through an art book I always carry with me. As I pondered Michelangelo's breath-taking Sistine Chapel painting overhead I was drawn to the Great Flood. Rather than vilifying those left behind to be drowned in the Flood while Noah's Blessed Community survived in the Ark, Michelangelo painted glimmers of holiness peeking from the sinners God had condemned to death. That's my message to you and your message to the Blessed Communities. We are not a network of little arks. God rejected that image right after the first – and the last - Flood. Love the sinners; love your enemies. Do good to those who persecute you. That's the message I'd have you pass on."

"And?"

"And if they get stuck see what others are doing. Keep in touch, celebrate the God's Kingdom on earth in this very generation."

"And if the violent ones would harm the innocent?"

"Let history play itself out. Others may take up arms to defend the innocent, but you are not to kill even to stop killing. You are called to be peacemakers, to be merciful, to be meek…"

"Not meek? Surely not meek."

"Jesus was meek. Like a lamb led to be slaughtered. Those who would follow him must not flinch before…"

"But…" Hans interrupted.

"But you must wrestle with that issue on your own Hans. Jesus walked this lonesome valley by himself and so must each one of us. So must each one of us…. Pax Vobiscom. Peace to all."

---

[8] Swiss presidents serve for one year with the option of serving again in the next election.

CHAPTER 14

OUR QUAKER THEOLOGIAN PONDERS THE OPTIONS

Meanwhile our perplexed Quaker theologian Hank Hangover is looking down at the little blue stick-it notes neatly lined up on the long polished mahogany table in one of the large conference rooms in Ludnick, the new Haverford library. How had the conflict between selective salvation versus universal salvation developed over time? Having spent the last three days after Christmas reaching credible generalizations based on diverse data Hank was on the verge of the critical insight he would soon share with Abbot Joel and the others. First he'd traced the events leading up to the Proud Boys' assassinating president Trump on Christmas Eve. Then the widespread natural and social chaos that followed, the pope's mysterious disappearance, the Blessed Communities in Berne, Peachtree and elsewhere, contentious discussions among Enrique Tarrio's Proud Boys leaked by renegade Jack, senator Dewlittle's neo-fascist Republicans, opportunistic ex-college president Sly Foxxy, and the two ardent Armageddon advocates, Pastor Jones and Q. Putting aside the history of the impending chaos spread out in little notes on the long table professor Hank stood up, rotated his aching shoulders, yawned, and waited for further inspiration.

"Closing time professor."

Hank looked up, sighed, and as he had many times before persuaded the late night librarian to leave him to his late night labors.

"*What now Lord*?" he thought to himself as he unpeeled the notes on the polished table, paused for thought, and wrote four new notes. Deep State. Armageddon. Kingdom. The Ring.

"*Deep State.*[9] *Deep State versus evidence. So many theories. Trump won the 2020 election. Climate change is a hoax. Covid-19 is another hoax. The economy, the media, the government are run by Deep State, a secret cabal of Satan worshiping child molesters. So many theories; so little evidence.*"

Pause.

Armageddon?

Pause.

Kingdom? Yes.

The Ring?

Power. Evil. Satan.

Back up Hank. Start from the beginning.

The Cloud of Knowing. Google.

Knowledge?

Knowledge in me.

Go on.

I'M GOOGLE!

Go on.

Yah!

Teeth clenched. Eyes wide.

Yah you shithead. You bastard. I hate your guts. Die shithead die.

Lord deliver me from Satan's wrath.

You are delivered Hank. Be at peace.

Pause.

Reflect. What happened? Step by step.

Knowledge out there led to knowledge in me. I drained Google. I became Google and my eyes grew wide, a harsh voice invaded my soul.

But....

But I have you Lord to bring me back.

And you learned?

---

[9] 5 Inner conversations and thoughts are written in italics.

Knowledge alone leads to power and power alone leads to the Angry One.

Pause.

And the Angry One leads to chaos which holds back your kingdom of justice and love; God's will on earth?

Yes Hank.

And we, those who do your will knowing and unknowingly, what should we do?

Small communities. Little families of love who care for one another and for one's enemies. Be campfires not just flashlights. Live the kingdom. Be God's people on earth blessed by the good spirit to love God and your neighbors. Pass it on to abbot Joel and the others.

After several minutes Hank smiled, gathered up the scraps of paper, said a quick prayer, turned out the lights, and slipped quietly out of Ludnick library.

***

When the little group of seven: the three Norbertines, and professor Hangover Hank from the States; Hale and Hearty Hannah, Hans, pope Philip, and Schatzi from Berne and Rome, settled into the two lumpy easy chairs and five old straight backs in room 1931 on the nineteenth floor of Margherita Suites, one of the less expensive hotels in Rome pope Philip responded to Dr. Hangover's unsettling suggestion that behind the wars, flooding and general chaos the spiritual conflict was between God and Satan.

"What you say professor may be true. I believe it is true, but I don't see how that matters. In fact the dangers of framing our conflict with Pastor Jones and his crowd in Satan versus God terms can only lead to a he-said she-said standoff. And eventually more blood-shed."

"I'm not suggesting we frame the conflict as Satan versus God, but I do think we might evoke the reality behind those two incendiary terms. At the spiritual level we might agree radical evil, the unseen will to kill, has incited murder, war, and genocide. We might also agree radiant goodness has enriched personal and even political life. Gandhi, Mother Teresa, and Dr. King inspired millions of ordinary citizens to face suffering and death, upgrading the natural love of spouse and family into political love of neighbor and enemy. Behind the visible skirmishes between chaos and compassion the unseen conflict between good and evil has been with us since Cain slew Abel."

Hans coughed. "Even if that's true; and most religious folks would agree, the problem is each side sees itself as morally superior to their enemies. Psychologists call this projection. Jesus called it hypocrisy. Your words he told the false scribes are…"

Woof?

"Projecting the evil in ourselves onto others. Personally and politically. Even a dog could…"

Woof!

"Politically means factions and nations.

Republicans, Trumpsters, and Democrats all proj…"

"Did you see that? The damn dog bit me."

When things settled the discussion moved on but Hans, the quick-witted but occasionally waspish stout lad, and dog world would not soon forget the unpleasant encounter.

Pope Philip drew the group into silence for a few minutes before opening the discussion on the way forward. After being assured the Blessed Communities were well formed and waiting for further directions from Rome, the pope asked for the group's response. Most had no leading beyond continuing to love their enemies no matter what. Even unto suffering and death, if it came to that, but Sister Phyllis' response was more specific.

"Perhaps we might match our enemies as they exist in small groups with our own small groups. Abbot Joel and one or two Norbertines might contact Senator Dewlittle. Peachbush Corries, Cohens, and Father Lopez might speak with Pastor Jones and his Armageddon army. Professor Hank might take on his crafty old boss ex-president Sly Foxxy. Arnold and Jack are already in contact with Enrique Tarrio, No. 1 Proud Boy. And your holiness could engage Q in a more enlightened bible study that doesn't involve God's killing off all the sinners who refused to acknowledge Jesus as Lord. And sending them to burn in Hell forever.

For a few moments no one spoke until Schatzi barked twice to confirm Sister Phyllis's suggestion. Faced with the specific tasks ahead Hank suggested a half hour reflection with IPads and notebooks on hand to gather their thoughts on ways to approach and love their organizational enemies.

After silence, song, and Sister Phyllis's final blessing, the group agreed to share their progress the following week three days after the New Year.

CHAPTER 15

THE GREAT DEBATE

At 10: 00 just after breakfast on January 3rd 20__+1 the little group of eight were reunited[10] in room 1931 at Margherita Suites. The room was overheated to compensate for the cold snap Rome was experiencing, but otherwise not much had changed. The straight back chairs were still hard on soft and flexible human backs; the two easy chairs reserved for pope Philip and Hannah Hossenhoeffer were lumpy and soft. The marguerites however, compliments of the house for special guests helped ease the group into the serious discussion they'd come for.

Deferring to president Hossenhoeffer as moderator the pope relaxed and prepared to take notes in his favorite forest green wide lined spiral notebook.

"Abbot Joel?"

Joel nods.

"Why don't we begin with your meeting with senator Dewlittle?"

Joel cleared his throat."

"It was a cordial meeting."

"How so?"

[10] Seven humans and one dog.

"I didn't tell him everything I knew and he didn't tell me everything he knew. We met on Zoom for about ten minutes."

"How did he respond to your calling for a joint effort to unite the country to deal with the flooding?"

"He said it reminded him of a fishing trip with a friend in Minnesota, he gave me a season's pass to the Astros home games, and six months supply of Texas beef."

"Did he say if he and his friend caught any fish?"

"The senator was very cordial but no, he didn't mention the fish again."

Pause. Sad sighs and Hannah moved on.

"Professor Hank?"

"I spoke with ex-president Foxxy, and his side kicks, coach Randelier and Tim Rottenburger for over an hour at the IHOP just off campus. I'd had several run-ins with the president when we were both working at the college, which we humorously referred to before I asked for his support in holding back the rising costal tides. Not personally but primarily through his connections to an unnamed trucking company, which could be useful in transporting supplies to stem the tide of coastal flooding. And several flood control companies. He sounded interested before casually mentioning he'd already had an offer from another interested party, and we spent the next half hour negotiating his cut, and coach Randy's and Tim's cut. I sensed he regretted bringing those two along, but it was a productive meeting and could be a real help. I didn't raise our deeper concern for fostering the Blessed Communities."

Woof?

"Because I wanted us to work on a common project before we moved into a closer relationship."

"Arnold? Jack? What's new with the Proud Boys? Enrique Tarrio is it?"

"Nothing they want to share with us. Enrique still has a fuckin' contract out on me. He then hung up on Arnold."

Woof..... outdoors...... Woof.

Twenty minutes passes and the discussion resumes.

"Hossie?"

"Yes mam?

"I'm a bit surprised the Peachbush bunch sent you."

Hossie blushed a tingly pink.

"We took a vote an' I won. Or lost dependin'. The Cohens and Father Lopez thought it should be a Corrie. Mama needs to care for poppa and poppa couldn't get off work."

"Was that all?"

"I guess they thought I'd do a good job."

"What's pastor Jones thinking?

"Pastor's changed. He were always a good ole southern preacher. Then he got the church goin' on Armageddon. Deacon Bestbuddy is worried 'bout Pastor Jones. He didn't say why but I could see pastor's eyes are different. Brighter, intense. It's scary. And he don't listen. Some folks think he's having another visit with the Holy Spirit but others like the deacon… well I don't rightly know what the deacon thinks but pastor Jones ain't the same, that's for sure."

Pause.

"Thank you Hossie. You're a very perceptive young man. If you lived in Berne you'd make a fine stout lad."

Then turning to the group she held out her hands and the group inched in closer and prayed for protection from Satan's presence in pastor Jones. "And in each one of us."

***

"You wanted to see me?"

Wearing a slim silver cross over his narrow Jesus Loves You tie Ron Watkins rumored by some to be Q himself smiled into the computer screen where Pope Philip, dressed in his papal robes, smiled back.

"I understand you have access to Q.?"

"What can I do for you Mr. Williams?"

"I'd like to talk with Q., without his having to reveal his identity if necessary. I was told you might arrange for a meeting to discuss an issue of interest to both of us."

"Which is?"

"It concerns Armageddon."

"Go on."

"As it stands now QAnon is committed to Armageddon as God's holy war against those who refuse to accept Jesus Christ as their Lord and Savior. They see myself and the church I represent as the Antichrist willfully rejecting God's holy will."

"Yes."

"Correct me if I'm wrong but QAnon has a two-fold mission. First to promote the Awakening when sinners realize global chaos: coastal flooding, wars and rumors of wars, etc., is God's holy war against Satan's Commie-liberal army on earth. And two the Storm which is the global chaos we're in now."

Ron nods.

"I and the church I represent take a different view, but we both have a common interest in saving as many sinners as possible from Satan's wrath. Would you agree?"

Again Ron nods.

"What's your proposal?"

"That Q and I go on global television and present our different views of the present chaos. Seen by the general public as a violent splinter group with crazy ideas about Democrats being a Satanic, baby killing, cult QAnon has a unique opportunity to respond to those charges."

"And from your point of view?"

"My hope would be to expose the general public to the threat groups like QAnon present to the civic welfare and to God's coming kingdom of justice and love."

***

Tuning in late after finishing the dinner dishes momma Corrie and Suzie Q were just in time for the end of CNN's Don Lemon's introduction to what was billed as The Final Fight for the Future featuring pope Philip and Q himself behind an Armageddon Now mask.

"… And in this corner wearing red robes and a gold tiara Pope Philip Neri. Gentlemen you know the rules. Each…."

Woof! WOOF!

Surprised to see the famous low slung long dog Schatzi on the tube momma Corrie turned up the sound to catch every word. In what? A bear trap? A lobster pot?

After a spirited but generally civil forty minute exchange of views Q's final remarks were another surprise.

"In closing I hope I've challenged the public perception of QAnon as an alt-right cult of violent religious fanatics. Like any group that challenges the status quo the media has misrepresented our movement. Like others we've had our traitors, our Judas Iscariots, but our mission has always been to be a peaceful prophetic voice for the Holy Spirit alerting humanity to God's coming Day of Judgement. The call to violence we've been accused of comes from scripture itself, and a few loose canons."

"What's a loose…"

"Not from QAnon's vindictiveness. Like Jesus we too love our enemies. Even Mr. Williams, with whom QAnon has irreconcilable differences, has presented his case in a thoughtful way.

In fact I believe Q has much in common with Mr. Williams's church. We both believe in God's bloody Day of Judgement, followed by God's kingdom on earth. May the God of Jacob, Isaac, and Jesus Christ be with you now and in the troubling times ahead."

"Pope Philip?"

"I sincerely wish I could believe Q's reconciling remarks. It's true we both believe natural and political chaos will usher in the last days before God's kingdom replaces our sin-saturated but also our love-blessed world, but before I continue I would ask that the five major networks[11] allow more time for Q and I to discuss our differences."

After a fifteen minute commercial break which included promos for cars, beer, whisky, adult diapers, sugary snacks, juicy hamburgers, comforting insurance plans, women's underwear, male perfume, and upcoming sit-coms and sports events, Don Lemon reported all the major networks had granted permission for the discussion to continue if… If QAnon and the Vatican would agree to pay for the programs and commercials bumped from the air to allow time for their continuing discussion. Having been prepared for the networks' financial concerns Q and the pope nodded their assent and the pope continued his closing remarks.

"St. Aquinas says Grace builds on Nature. Nature being the goodness given to every human being at their birth. In other words the creation can't be totally corrupted by human sin."

Cough. Hack. Sneeze.

---

[11] ABC, CBS, NBC, Fox News, and CNN.

"I'm not sure where this is heading Holy Father. What's Aquinas got to do with Armageddon?"

"If Aquinas's thinking is right God would not condemn anyone who dies in Armageddon to eternal damnation. To death perhaps but not to eternal damnation. Aquinas says, God will "complete the creation to God's satisfaction" and a loving God could not be satisfied if even one of God's children were to suffer eternal damnation. Since there's much good in the worst of us St. Aquinas's logic would not, I believe, condemn anyone to eternal damnation."

Q's eyes crinkled.

"How then do you account for the fact that Aquinas *did* believe in eternal damnation?"

"Faulty logic. His narrow view of Purgatory which grants eventual salvation to some sinners and not others is not consistent with a loving God who cares for all God's children."

"You do know there's precious little biblical evidence for purgatory."

"Yes but I don't think all the world's wisdom got into the bible. I don't know many saints who are ready for heaven at the time of their death; nor do I know many sinners deserving of eternal damnation at the time of their death."

"Jack the Ripper? Attila the Hun? Those who torture helpless fellow human beings? Adolf Hitler?"

"A critical, perhaps unresolvable theological issue. Scripture, intentionally perhaps, leaves the relationship between God's forgiveness and God's justice as an unresolved issue."

"As it should be for us? An individual matter, Holy Father?"

"Yes. That's God's issue Don. Ours is to do good to those who persecute us. To love our enemy as we love our own bodies. For us to condemn anyone even Hitler to eternal damnation would be to play God. God has God's role; we humans have ours."

"But forgiving Hitler, especially for those who survived the death camps, is not humanly possible."

"When the Dalai Lama asked a fellow monk, who'd been imprisoned by the Chinese invaders for twenty years, what he feared most in prison, the monk said his greatest fear was that he would come to hate his abusive jailors."

"Twenty years in prison is still not the Holocaust."

"Shortly after being released from Ravenbruck, a Nazi death camp in northern Germany created largely for Communist women, Corrie ten Boom, a Dutch survivor, was preaching in Munich on forgiveness. After the service, greeting the congregation as they were leaving, Corrie saw the guard from Ravenbruck, who'd watched while she and her sister were forced to undress as they entered the camp. When the guard approached and asked for forgiveness Corrie froze and turned away. As she prayed to Jesus to soften her heart she was filled with compassion for the former death camp guard. Later Corrie said those who could forgive their former oppressors went on to happier lives. Those who could not forgive were burdened with what Dr. King called the 'fatigue of bitterness, and the drain of resentment.'"

"Holy Father, could we get back to Armageddon?"

Brrrrrrrrrrrrrring. Brrrrrrrrrrrrrrring.

Mizz Corrie clicked off the T.V. to answer the phone.

"Hello?"

….. …… ……….###***@@@@### …… ………. **%%%.******

Click.

"Who was it momma?"

"Another one of those calls."

"Did you recognize the voice?"

"It sounded like Harry who lives two doors down. The one you used to go fishing with… O Fred I don't think I can take it anymore. All our old…" Sobbing, eyes running with tears, chest heaving, hands clenched mizz Corrie finally wiped her eyes and looked up.

"Sorry love. Sometimes it gets to me… Now what would you like for dinner? Just you, me, and Suzy Q."

CHAPTER 16

THE TIDE COMES IN

The next day the great crowd that had come to the festival (Passover) heard that Jesus was coming to Jerusalem. So they took branches of palm trees and went out to meet him shouting, "Hosanna!

Blessed is the one who comes in the name of the Lord – the king of Israel." John 12: 12-13.

***

National Catholic Reporter

It seems only yesterday Dallas Bishop Strickland was commending Wisconsin Father James Altman for his no bullshit, in your face, straight from the shoulder, tell it like it is, take no prisoners, straight talk. Speaking to "clueless baptized Catholics… My shame is it's taken me so long. Thank you Father Altman for your COURAGE" in condemning fellow priest F. Martin, from wouldn't you know it, Satin's city, the poisonous Big Apple. To Hell. Along with millions of Democrats who'll be joining Father

Martin for the "mortal sin" of "voting for Biden." But there is a way out. "Repent of your support for that party and its platform or face the fires of hell."

However! However despite continuing chaos and rabid rhetoric there is light on the horizon. In Texas of all places. Norbertine Abbot Joel from Daylesford Abbey, Pennsylvania, reports that after a three hour conference and confession with Texas' neo-fascist Republican senator Darlington Dewlittle, the good senator agreed to vote with the progressive Democrats on changing climate change, help for welfare mothers, and a 90% tax on all millionaires and a 97% tax on all billionaires to pay for Build Back Better III.

While Abbot Joel could not of course reveal what was said in the confessional, he and senator Dewlittle held a press conference in which Darlington as he called himself, would only say he'd had a change of heart and was leaving the Republican party to run as a Dr. King Democrat in the upcoming election.

Following the senator's remarkable change of heart five other Republican senators, fourteen congresswomen and seven congressmen from the Trump infested Republican party issued a joint statement saying "Enough is enough."

Wow! Whoa! Whoopee! In the next three weeks the political floodgates of living love opened. The president's Soak The Rich, STR, tax bill passed both houses easily; vaccines, booster shots, and mask wearing in public became mandatory; urban block parties and rural hoedowns, and the entire list of liberal proposals would be funded by the STR tax bill. The president's public works projects reduced unemployment by ninety percent, leaving stay-at-home single parents, welfare caregivers, and unpublished authors free to fill their appointed roles in the truly great society.

***

Back in the just off campus IHOP our two featured academics, Dr. Foxxy and professor Hank, were into their second cup of expresso when Dr. Foxxy put down his fork and looked across the hard linoleum table top at his adversarial colleague.

"How didit go?"

"Your acceptance speech last week on national T.V?"

"Do you think the audience bought it?"

"Your heart felt conversion to Jesus? And being honored to be chosen as the president's new press secretary? You know the polls were good. Why ask me?"

"You know me, Hank. We don't always agree on political..."

"Hardly ever... You want my real opinion?"

"I do."

"I think you lived up to your name. Sly Foxxy. But I also think you're the right man for the job. Americans love repentant rascals. 'Ex-con served his time, found Jesus and wants to serve his country. Articulate, engaging, great fundraiser.' I think you'll do fine if..."

"If I don't switch back to the old Foxxy?"

"I don't worry about that. The way the country's swung back to Bernie Sanders and Gandhi I don't think you'll risk another life-changing transformation."

Pause.

"Why not?"

"I don't see you driven by power. Getting your cut is what motivates you old friend."

"Old friend?"

"Why not? We're both getting on.... I'm pleased for you Sly. Is that really your name?"

"My given name's Sylvester, but after selling phony lottery tickets in junior high, those with a nose for dodgy dealings stuck me with Sly. It's been with me ever since, More coffee?"

Hank shakes his head. Awkward silence.

"I seem to have left my credit cards at home."

"So have I... Sly."

***

Meanwhile the Proud Boys' top brass known as the Fuckin' Fourteen currently chaired by Enrique Tarrio, were meeting in the conference room at Cabana Boise the shabby, and cheapest hotel, in downtown Boise.

"Everyone have a fuckin'g copy?"

Pause for response.

"Good."

"Enrique man?"

"Yeah?"

"I thought this was supposed to be a closed meeting. What's Jack doing here? With a fuckin' snowflake."

"Jack's been reinstated. He and his visitor have a few words for us."

"###@@*****...... Jack's a fuckin'.... ++++%%

%%##..... fuckin'....%&#*.....!

"Shut the fuck up and listen. Then vote me out if you want. OKAY?"

As the Fuckin' Fourteen slowly settled down Tarrio, the only Proud Boy allowed to smoke, lit his smelly Cuban short cigar, cleared his throat, inhaled briefly, and spat on the shiny wood floor in the...

"As you assholes may have noticed the mood of the country has changed. The fuckin' liberals are in charge and like it or not the country's doin' well. New roads and bridges; the old 'Biden viruses'; are dropping every month; coastal flooding has receded – Long Island beaches are open for business; I Love Lucy, Gandhi, and Babbit's Feast have driven high tech end of the world thrillers off the air; and the US is a top five nation in the Bhutan National Happiness annual report.

So where does that leave the Proud Boys? Let's be honest. We've lost our base. Our last attack on the Lincoln Memorial went nowhere. Outnumbered five to one by counter demonstrators BLM and their ilk, we never got within three blocks of the Memorial. Five of our boys are in jail for attempted murder and one for breaking a cop's leg. Facebook and social media won't accept our ads and the media coverage has been brutal."

"But we're never mentioned not even on Fox News."

"That's what's brutal."

"So that's it? We disband? Melt back into the mob?"

Enrique smiled, cleared his throat, and spat on the shiny hard wood well-worn caramel colored floor again and ...

"Quit? Not on your ass. Our base is still out there. Subdued but available when the incoming tide of good times rolls back out to sea leaving behind the barren beach."

"Mixin' metaphors aren't you 'Rique? When Long Island's underwater it's a peaceful beach invaded by an angry ocean; now it's the ocean of love covering the barren beach."

"Metaphors work both…"

"So I asked Jack back and his liberal friend, Arnold Really O'Reilly, to explain our next move. Listen to what they have to say. If you don't like it vote me out. Ok?"

Nods and shrugs signal assent.

Jack looked around the room till he has everyone attention.

"I see you all have *From Chaos to Christ: the new non-violence* by Enrique Tarrio and Arnold Really O'Reilly based on the gospel of Matthew. Good. The Proud Boys rebranded as the Baptized Boys, who love Jesus and follow the Sermon on the Mount, will be our new image. We'll be back in the news for running a soup kitchen in Harlem and prison workshops that introduce violent and psychotic prisoners to the virtues of Christian non-violence. To our old fans, quietly contacted one-on-one, we're still the Proud Boys dedicated to taking back America."

Scattered discussion punctuated with colorful language was generally positive.

"Great idea but why would you" looking at their liberal visitor, "support operation Trojan Horse?"

Arnold, a lean six four with deep set dark eyes, a rosy scar across his left cheek, and wispy grey-white hair on top paused before responding.

"Frankly it raises an issue that could go either way. Perhaps the impact of the Proud Boys' conversion will outlast their later cancelled conversion. Perhaps the heroic ethos of nonviolence will appeal to your zealous nature; your inner anger pressing for a better world. Perhaps the Trojan Horse *will* unleash chaos, but that's a risk I'm willing to take. Besides I enjoy working with Enrique, except for those God awful Cuban cigars."

***

Meanwhile back in Peachbush Pastor Jones had retired from public life. Confused and discouraged by the liberal-laced ocean of love that put at risk his beloved Armageddon Pastor Jones went back to the desert, just as Jesus had, for six months to seek the Father's will. At his farewell service the good pastor expressed undying love for his beloved congregation and asked for their prayers that the Holy Spirit would bless God's humble servant with a renewed vision for the Lily White Church in the Valley.

Two weeks later Pastor Jones showed up for the 9:00 o'clock Sunday service. Smiling!? When the opening hymn and readings had finished Pastor Jones stepped to the pulpit. Now in his early 60's, dressed informally in light tan shorts and a skimmer red beaked short sleeved shirt half the congregation missed his Jesus Loves You wide purple and pink tie and half welcomed their smiling, light touch pastor who looked to bring good news from the desert.

"My friends, and truly you are my friends, when I left I had planned on six months away, but after a week of eating well, napping, sleeping, reading scripture and old Nero Wolfe mysteries my inner angry subsided. My body and mind were at peace but two days later peace had morphed into boredom and I was as restless as a nervous newt, or miz Laird fighting to stay awake during one of my longer sermons."

"What? What'd he say? Did I hear my name mentioned?"

"Hush grannie; I'll tell you later." And so the good pastor went on with the sermon.

"Sitting alone on the porch of Old Smoky Lodge in the Smoky Mountains I heard an inner voice unlike any I'd heard before, say 'Follow me.'"

"Where Lord? Where would you lead me?"

"Away from Satan and all his works."

As I sat staring at the dark-green pines that encircled the hotel, the grey gravel driveway, the parked cars in front, and the far faint blue sky above I waited for the voice to continue, but the voice was silent. I was itching to leave but something kept me riveted to the old mountain oak rocker, staring into space until I heard myself saying, "Yes Lord… Yes, I renounce Satan and all his evil works."

Reliving the memory, pastor Jones mopped his brow with his old red handkerchief lowered his head and wept. Then lifting his face he spoke the words his congregation would remember as long as they lived.

"Dear friends I was wrong. I was led astray by the evil one. Forgive me." Putting his arms out his flushed face streaming with tears, pastor Jones came out from the behind the pulpit and knelt on well-worn wooden boards in front of the crowded benches until his friends came forward and embraced their broken pastor.

Several minutes passed in silence until the choir master asked pastor Jones for a closing song. Looking up the good pastor whispered, "Jesus walked this lonesome valley." When the singing was over everyone got up and left the church quietly.

***

The next day Pastor Jones made two phone calls. One to Father Lopez to ask for forgiveness and arrange for the two churches to worship together in the high school gymnasium on Helen Keller's birthday. As a revered southern hero blind Helen Keller[12], whose life symbolized light in the midst of darkness, appealed to Pastor Jones' lily white congregation as well as Father Lopez's brown-skinned Latino flock.

The second call was to invite the Corries and rabbi Cohen's family to a barbeque by Lakelovers lake two miles from Peachbush itself. Many folks of course thought Pastor Jones was moving too fast. Christian fellowship was something to work toward; something that preserved the sensibilities of each tradition. When a small committee of leading citizens visited the good pastor Rufus Jones agreed he was moving faster than he'd intended, but said God seemed to be impatient to bring his children together.

***

"Joyful, joyful we adore thee God of glory God of love, Hearts unfold like flowers before Thee opening to the sun above... "

"Bueno dias. Bon jour. Halo. Good morning. Gute Morge. You've reached the pope's answering service."

Two minutes later abbot Joel from Daylesford abbey in the states had pope Philip Neri on the line. After several minutes of small talk on health and the weather in Rome and southeast Pennsylvania the pope asked abbot Joel what was going on with what was being called the American Miracle.

"Bob it's amazing. Pastor Jones and senator Dewlittle have had a complete of change of heart; Foxxy and the Proud Boys are at least

[12] Helen Keller despite being blind all her life was an honored champion for human rights including of course the blind. Her books, public appearances here and abroad, and her warm and courageous personality appealed to fellow southerners and to northern liberals including socialists.

publically supportive. The Holy Spirit's clearly been at work. Pray God it continues."

Pause.

"Bob?"

"Yes."

"Were you able to contact Q?"

"I talked with several higher ups who are close to Q but I was never able to talk with Q himself."

CHAPTER 17

CHAOS

"Pilate, wanting to release Jesus, addressed them again; but they kept shouting, "Crucify, crucify him!" A third time he said to them, "Why, what evil has he done?"... But they kept urgently demanding with loud voices that he should be crucified; and their voices prevailed." Luke: 23: 20-23.

Looking back there is no consensus on when the tide began to turn. Some pointed to the forest fires in Oregon and east coast hurricanes; some to the Miami Herald article that Florida governor "Unmask America/ The Right to Bare Arms" Ron de Santis; and QAnon congresswoman Marjorie Taylor Greene sniping at one another over who should head the ticket in the next presidential election; and some to QAnon's social media claim that Dr. Fauci's vaccines are microscopic extraterrestrials sent from outer space to depopulate planet Earth.

Whatever the initial turning point it was clear the Four Horsemen of the Apocalypse: War, Famine, Death, and the Anti-Christ were abroad in the land. Call it the Apocalypse or Armageddon, the last days before the end of the world are upon us. The great suffering; what St. Paul called the "groaning creation" swept over the planet. Hospital staff: nurses, doctors, orderlies, and paramedics ran into the streets crazed by grief for a pandemic they could no longer contain leaving patients moaning and screaming for respirators and pain-killers that never came. Torrential rains grounded the planes, trains, and trucks that brought food into the cities around the world: Lima, Bueno Aires, London and Paris, St. Petersburg, Philadelphia, Delhi, Istanbul, Sao Paulo, Bethlehem, Cape Town, Lagos, and Albuquerque. Smaller cities and towns close to farms and orchards; rivers, lakes and oceans fared slightly better, but everywhere food and water were fought over or shared. And somewhere above the groaning creation the second horseman Famine rode on, searching for signs of serenity.

As sickness and starvation ravaged the land wars broke out. At first the wars were waged by nations competing for food or settling old grievances, but the violence quickly spread to the adversarial factions within each nation: rich versus poor, white versus black and brown, straight vs. anyone not straight, Democrats versus other Democrats, Trumpsters versus everybody else, Hindu versus Muslim, Buddhist versus Hindu and Muslim, nationalist Hindus versus Gandhian Hindus, Christians versus Muslims, Evangelical Christians versus main stream and liberal believers, liberals versus main stream Christians, traditional pope John Paul II Catholics versus Vatican II John XXII Catholics, liberal General Conference Quakers versus conservative Friends in Ohio, Iowa, North Carolina and FUM, Friends United Meeting. Small f friend versus friend. Parents versus children. Sibling versus sibling. Husband versus wife.

Everyday exchanges led to arguments and name calling. Name calling to insults; insults to pushing, shoving, punches and sometimes death. Adversarial groups banded together to defend their identity with arguments, demonstrations, violence, and bloodshed. Grieving their fallen heroes each side returned to the conflict lusting for revenge.

Chaos reigned. War the second horseman, like Tolkein's Night Riders, the deadly Nazguls, folded into QAnon's Armageddon.

Pause.

"And the AntiChrist?"

"Secluded in the shadows."

CHAPTER 18

FEAR AND GREAT JOY

"After the Sabbath, as the first day of the week was dawning, Mary Magdalene and the other Mary went to see the tomb. And suddenly there was a great earthquake; for an angel of the Lord descending from heaven... said to the women, "Do not be afraid; I know that you are looking for Jesus who was crucified. He is not here; for he has been raised... So they left the tomb quickly with fear and great joy, and ran to tell his disciples." Matthew 28.

"Poppa."

"Yes?"

"Does going to Father Lopez's church make us Catholics?'

"Not yet. We'll have to see. Why? Are you thinking of becoming a Catholic?"

"No. I was just wonderin' since Father Lopez's church was blown away in the tornado they couldn't meet in the high school gym with Pastor Jones' congregation; like we did that one time six months ago? The two pastors could combine the two services, and we could clear the floor after church twice a month and let the under twenty teens, play the old guys..."

Woof!!
"And gals."

***

Navajo Times Editorial
Mother Earth Near Death

Six months ago it seemed Mother Earth would survive the horrors of war and famine. Two thirds of Indian land seized by the white man had been returned to its rightful owners. Financial restitution in the millions allowed Native Americans to raise their young as Christians and Jews do, in the ways of their ancestors. Ecumenical pow-wows had sprung up in Canada and all fifty states. Indian pottery, flutes, drums, and moccasins were selling well, and Native American history was included in the curriculum of thirty five of the fifty one states.

Today things have changed. The Four Horsemen are back. The land is parched and barren. The forests have been swept by fire; water covers the land a hundred miles inland on both coasts. Tornados twist and swirl their way across the middle states. The medicine men are weeping.

O dear Mother we pray for your recovery. Have mercy on your children. Wakan Tanka, Great Spirit, send rain to the parched middle earth and lift the waters from sky and seas that would cover the coastlines.

***

Perched uncomfortably with his back against the wall on the top row of Peachbush Jefferson Davis Memorial High School Hossie Corry scratched the outside of his left nostril and tried to make out the foremost figures on the far floor below. Father Lopez in his violet and white advent vestment was talking with Pastor Jones in his dark blue suit and red tie; white-haired prim and portly Terry Tunes was at the piano off to the side, and the interdenominational purple and gold gowned choir standing behind the two pastors were waiting patiently for the service to begin. The stands were sparsely filled on both sides of the court; not with the happy expectation of beating a hated rival, but with a desperate longing for relief from the whirling chaos that had destroyed half the homes and public buildings in town, including Piggly Wiggly and mizz Thompson's Peachbush Pantry, where people got their food. People were hungry, children were crying for food; water was scarce. After the opening readings and hymns Father Lopez stepped to the pulpit.

"My friends let us pray."

Pause.

"Lord deliver your people from the whirling winds that have decimated our homes and stores. And if you cannot hold back the devastating storms give your people comfort and courage in our hour of need. Please God hear our prayer."

After repeating his prayer in Spanish Father Lopez sat down and covered his face in his hands.

After a few minutes Pastor Jones stood up and when he'd had several strong members of the choir remove the pulpit he turned and pointed to the stands behind him.

"Rabbi Cohen," he called up, "Would give us your blessing?"

Taken by surprise the good rabbi who was sitting half way up in the stands said a few words in Yiddish to his son Sam and the two made their way to the floor below.

Standing with the two Christian pastors rabbi Cohen said a few words in Hebrew which Sam, his curly black-haired Yamaha topped teenaged son, translated for the crowd.

"My father thanks Pastor Jones for inviting him to speak." Then handing the microphone to his father Sam stepped back. When the rabbi had finished his short prayers in Hebrew he handed the mike back to his son.

"My father quoted two prayers from the Tanakh."

"The what?" Someone called out.

"The Hebrew bible. The first is from psalm 6: 2.

"O Lord, heal me, for my bones are shaking with terror." When Sam finished Hossie, and many around the small gym, opened their wordless mouths in anguish. Trembling with fear. But as Sam quoted the second prayer "*Then they cried to the Lord in their trouble, and he sent out his word and he saved them from their distress. He sent out his word and he healed*

them." rabbi Cohen lifted his head, raised his arms and smiled up at the scattered crowd above.

***

As K lay dying on the cold stone streets of Munich he turned his head and with his last breath he saw on the top floor of the dark building above one lighted window.

CHAPTER 19

DID GOD FORGIVE HITLER?

O Lord, you God of vengeance shine forth! Rise up, O judge of the earth; give the proud what they deserve. O Lord how long shall the wicked exult?... They crush your people and afflict your heritage. They kill the widow and the stranger, they murder the orphan, and they say "the Lord does not see; the God of Jacob does not perceive." Ps. 94 1-7

Whoever disobeys the Son will not see life, but must endure God's wrath. Jn. 3:35

"Vengeance is mine. I will repay." Hebrews 10: 30

Meanwhile in Rome Bob Williams was sitting alone in the Sistine Chapel on a folding chair staring up at Michelangelo's Last Judgement. Christ in the middle welcomes saints on his right hand into the joys of heaven; condemning sinners on his left to the eternal torments of Hell. As pope Philip Neri, Holy Father to well over two billion believers, had never been troubled by God's condemning a sizable portion of humanity to Hell. Justice must be served in the afterlife as well as on earth, but as Bob

William, altar boy from Albuquerque, New Mexico, his heart was troubled. How could a loving God even think of such wickedness? Hadn't Jesus preached we were to love our enemies; to pray for those who persecuted us? Hadn't he died forgiving those who killed him: soldiers, a reluctant Roman governor, Temple tending Sadducees, and the mobs who cried out for the death of the rabblerousing heretic from Galilee?

Commending his troubled soul into the arms of God Bob Williams – alias Pope Philip – quietly wept his way back into God's love and guidance, until the chapel grew dim and it was time to return to his responsibilities.

***

FLASHBACK TO APRIL 30th 1945.

In a tastefully furnished medium-sized sitting room in the underground Fuhrerbunker Adolf Hitler was seated beside his new bride, Eva Braun. They should have been holding hands and smiling; planning for their honeymoon and life together. There should have been chocolate eclairs and candy bars to enhance Hitler's vegetarian diet, and perhaps the Goebbels family who lived a few doors away would drop in to celebrate with the happy couple.

As Hitler looked up at the fine portrait of his hero the warrior iron man, Prussian king Fredrick the Great, his mind was filled with hatred for his encircling enemies: Communist swine hunting him down through the streets of Berlin, Goring the traitor who'd tried to take over Germany, and Germany itself who had betrayed their Fuhrer by losing the war. Fingering the sleek compact Walther PRK pistol in his pocket the new bridegroom could see El Duce's dead body in Milan hanging by its heels. Not for me. Not for me and Hitler handed his bride the cyanide pill swallowed his own, put the gun to his right temple and pulled the trigger.

***

Eyes pinned wide against the burning light Hitler, howling for death heard a voice within the light; saw a figure sitting on the judge's throne. His eyes throbbing with pain Adolf listened to the judge's list, as images of his former life flashed upon his inner eye. SS Commander Ernest Rohm, his former friend, shot in his cell on Hitler's command. The human pyramid of slippery naked bodies; young and old, women, men, and children, clawing their way upward over one another inhaling lethal gas. Eleven million human beings gassed on Hitler's implied[13] command. Millions upon millions, soldiers and civilians, killed in the war and still Hitler held to his belief in his sacred destiny to rid the world of vermin to initiate a thousand years of love and peace and joy on earth.

Eyes still fierce with hatred Hitler faced his tormentor; the Jew upon the throne of God.

"Adolf?"

"It is I."

"You know what you have done?"

"Judge me as you will; I'd do it again."

"You loved your mother?"

"I did."

"And Eva Braun?"

"Yes."

"And the German people."

"Until they betrayed my trust."

"You do know the case against you is strong?"

Silence.

"Nevertheless dear Adolf I forgive you."

***

National Enquirer

God Forgives Hitler?

Just in from Peachbush Ga., Suzi Q Corrie, an otherwise normal and certifiably sane, thirteen year old teenager claims she had a vision that Adolf Hitler had been forgiven by the Higher Power. Neighbors and school mates testified in an ongoing investigation into Suzi's mental health that aside from her extraordinary claim Suzi Q was a shy, good-hearted,

[13] Hitler never officially ordered the Holocaust. This was done by others aware of Hitler's intent who carried out Hitler's wishes. This was known as "Working Toward Hitler." Without Hitler there is no Holocaust

intelligent teenager. Her family, had no comment except for her older brother Jehosaphat Corrie who said "If Suzi said it I believe it."

National Catholic Reporter

Rome. Under intense questioning pope Philip conceded that he would be conferring with a diverse group of trusted advisors including archbishop Gomez president of the USCCB, United States Conference of Catholic Bishops, on multiple reports of God forgiving Hitler. His Holiness said he would get back to the press with an interim report by next Thursday. The pope said "These things take time. The theological implications alone are earthshaking; not to mention the effect on everyday Catholic behavior." The pontiff ended the interview asking laity and clergy to pray for the group that would be discerning God's will on this critical issue.

***

Secluded alone in the smallest conference room in the Vatican the pope turned on his computer and in a few seconds was looking at the boxed faces of seventeen of his most trusted advisors. After twenty minutes of silent prayer His Holiness Bob Williams from Albuquerque asked the group whether Suzi Q Corrie's vision, and the fifteen other collaborating visions, were credible. Everyone agreed Suzi Q and the others thought they'd had a genuine vision but Archbishop Gomez, Rabbi Cohen, and Hans Yodelgruber argued scripture clearly claimed God was a God of justice who did send unrepentant sinners to hell. Justice demands a deadline; it doesn't go on unresolved forever. Death is God's deadline.

All the others including Swiss ex-president Hannah Hossenhoeffer, Senator Dewlotts, chubby teen Hossie Jehosaphat Corrie, ex-Proud Boy Enrique Tarrio, and pastor Jones argued for, or intuitively believed, that God was a God of everlasting love – no matter what – quoting Jesus's Sermon ("love your enemy, pray for those who persecute you") and *First Corinthians 13* where love is greater than all knowledge, prophetic powers, and spiritual mysteries.

Enrique and Darlington Jones mindful of their own forgiveness hesitated to cut short God's forgiveness even for sinners like Jack the Ripper,

Attila the Hun, and Hitler. Rabbi Cohen and Hans of course argued that God's forgiveness was dependent on repentance. To include unrepentant sinners as part of God's family would divide the family against itself, and sin would spread all over again. This silenced the love conquers all crowd momentarily, and the discussion moved on.

His Holiness sneezed, scrunched his shoulders and asked if everyone was ready for a break. Sensing no objections the pope turned off Zoom and went to the Sistine Chapel with a ham sandwich, a bottle of Lowenbrau and a cannoli for desert. When the group reconvened after lunch the pope turned to Abbot Joel.

"Abbot Joel, we haven't heard from the Norbertines. What's their response to Jesus forgiving Hitler?"

Joel looked over at Sister Phyllis.

"I accept Suzi Q's vision as a genuine word from the Holy Spirit to God's church. I believe we are being called to love our enemies unconditionally. That's what Gandhi and Dr. King did. If mere mortals could forgive their enemies why wouldn't God? A.J. Muste Quaker leader of the anti-war movement in the 1960s told us "If you can't love Hitler you can't love anybody." That's what a lot of us have tried to do. How Christian nonviolence fits into God's overall plan for the coming Kingdom of God is not our concern. Like good servants we do what we're told and leave the rest to God."

Having as a courtesy left archbishop Gomez, president of the American bishops' conference until last, that he might comment on what had been said before, pope Philip gestured toward his old nemesis who smiled and began to read a prepared statement.

"Anticipating the responses we've just heard I've been advised by a substantial majority of American bishops to defend the teaching of the Church, which has never seriously questioned God's judgement on the unrighteous. *Genesis 19: 24, 25* records that for their sins 'the Lord rained on Sodom and Gomorrah sulfur and fire from the Lord out of heaven.' Four thousand years later (from the destruction of Sodom and Gomorrah in 2070 B.C.E. to 2021 C.E.) God's judgement on the wicked has not altered one iota. In *Matthew 25: 41, 46* Jesus addresses the wicked ones, 'You that are accursed depart from me into the eternal fire prepared for the devil and his angels… [for you] will go away into eternal punishment, but the righteous into eternal life.' In light of Church teaching which adheres closely to sacred scripture the American bishops maintain that Hitler is safely in Hell where he belongs."

As Bob Williams listened to archbishop Gomez read his carefully prepared statement, the gist of which he'd heard a thousand times, but 'neer so well expressed' the word 'Wicked' exploded in his mind and soul.

Looking up at the boxed faces on the screen in front of him he sensed he was not alone in his reservations, and after thanking the archbishop for his thoughtful contribution, the pope called for another Zoom meeting at 8:00 in the evening, Central European Time.

***

The pope's eight o'clock Zoom meeting, considering the issues involved, was fairly short. The introductory issue was whether scripture and Catholic tradition allowed for Continuing Revelation to enhance Closed Revelation [the Crucifixion, the Resurrection, the Trinity and God's Kingdom on earth] IE could God's punitive judgement be modified by biblical love and forgiveness? Could murderous tyrants like Hitler, be forgiven, even after death? The Norbertines and pastor Sophia and her husband, dog master deacon Lance Lott, argued that many church teachings *had* changed over the centuries.

Many scholars argued that though slavery had been controversial throughout the Church's history it was not until 1890, or perhaps as late as Vatican II in the 1960s that Rome definitively outlawed slavery. Throughout the Greco-Roman, medieval, and modern eras papal teaching wavered between condemnation and acceptance. The critical distinction between "justified and unjustified slavery" died hard in the Catholic church where millions of Spanish, Portuguese, and American Catholics did hold slaves.

The Church's retraction of its teachings on Galileo's astronomy and Darwinian evolution were other examples of the Church changing its mind on critical issues. Renouncing burning and hanging heretics, after almost four hundred years from the late eleventh to the mid fifteenth century was the most overdue retraction of all papal-supported practices. It's no wonder Luther and the early Protestants and Antipapists railed against the pope as the Anti-Christ.

On the positive side many saints like Francis and Clare of Assisi, Teresa of Avila and Catherine of Sienna, Dorothy Day, Mother Teresa, and Pope John XXIII were blessed with revelations which challenged abuses in the Church, and enlivened the faithful with a renewed heart for social justice and God's love. The question today is whether God's justice is tit for tat, eye for eye, legal justice or family justice which seeks to restore the sinner to his or her place in God's human family. In heaven if not on earth.

When pastor Sophia and deacon Lance finished archbishop Gomez, said the sins of the Church, even papal sins, which raised another controversial issue, were incidental, leaving Closed Revelation unscathed.

Given the obvious deadlock between Closed and Continuing Revelation someone suggested - it may have been senator Darlington Dewlotts who was getting on in years –that they all get a good night's sleep and continue in the morning, evening or afternoon depending on where one was Zooming from.

***

Meanwhile somewhere in Washington state Ron Watkins, rumored to be the mysterious "Q" of QAnon was doodling on his yellow pad and reflecting on the options available.

1. Lay low until clear signs of Satanic activity surface[14] in socio-political national and global affairs.
2. Concentrate on the Anti-Christ in Rome.
3. Contact fellow believers. Oath Keepers, Proud Boys left after Tarrio defected, Holocaust deniers, New World Warriors armed for imminent insurrection.
4. Take over the cryptocurrency market to confuse and replace the current monetary system.

---

[14] QAnon is an alt-right conspiracy theory that claims Satanic pedophiles are running a global child-trafficking ring. They use website 8chan to spread their views, and were publicly active in the January 6, 2021 insurrection challenging Biden's election. Later they accepted the legitimacy to Biden's election. Despite QAnon's claim to expose Satanism, "Q" himself is secretly committed to Satan's cause. His followers however are motivated by the common projection of their own inner evil onto their innocent enemy.

5. Randomly assassinate non-white public figures in the three branches of government at the national and state level; in the arts, media; and sports.
6. Check with dad before taking action.

CHAPTER 20

PURGATORY

Woof. woof woof. .... Arf!

Interrupted by Schatzi's barking half way through the mandatory opening twenty minute quiet time the pope enlarged dog master Lance Lott's image on the screen and asked for a translation.

"Schatzi says she's conferred with the dogs and they agree Hitler's not ready for heaven even though he's been forgiven by God. They suggest Hitler needs to be rehabilitated before he's open to repentance."

Cough. Cough.

Hans. "It's assumed then that everyone will repent?"

"Not at all. Repentance is an option; not a requirement. People aren't robots, especially in God's homeland."

Pause.

Hossie. "Do the dogs have a suggestion on how Hitler might be saved? He sure needs to be rehabilitated but he weren't a Buddhist, who depends on reincarnation for their eventual salvation."

"As a baptized and confirmed lapsed Catholic Hitler still had access to the trials and tribulations of purgatory. Purgatory not as punishment, but purgatory as therapy under the care of a skilled and loving counselor has the sinner relive and reevaluate the critical events in their past. T.S.Eliot's

'[You've] had the experience but missed the meaning'. Perhaps one's guardian angel acts as a loving counselor. Or Jesus, Mary or a saving figure from one's own religious past. Mohammed, Kuan Yin bodhisattva Mother of Mercy for Buddhists, and Chinese peasants.'"

"So you're saying repentance is still possible even after death?"

"Yes.

"But Protestants say purgatory isn't even mentioned in the bible."

Woof...... .... WOOF!

"The dogs say stop now; this could go on forever. They're worried about the world."

"Aren't we all."

CHAPTER 21

THE LAST CHAPTER

Straightening the yellow pad by his side pope Philip clicked on his Zoom web portal, waited for all seventeen boxed faces to appear and after a few minutes of stillness addressed his trusted advisors. "As this may be our last Zoom meeting I would appreciate your considered opinion on what lies ahead for humanity in this troubled time. Let's start with the youngest."

Suzi Q blushed and put her head down until her older brother Hossie nudged her to speak up.

"I think everything will be fine. I don't know much about the bible but if God's in charge he won't let it end any other way."

Archbishop Gonzalez waited a few minutes and repeated his claim that Christ on the Day of Judgement would separate the sheep from the goats sending saints to heaven and sinners to hell.

Ex-Proud Boys Enrique and Jack said they were still easing their way into the Christian life and didn't have a considered opinion on how the world ends.

Arnold, the mystery writer from Maine, agreeing with Enrique and Jack, said he does the best he can and leaves the rest to God. He said he hoped he'd have time to finish his latest manuscript, The Rusty Revolver. And that there would be people left to read it. Ex-madam president Hannah

Hossenhoeffer and her two stout lads in Berne, Wiggy and Hans offered a joint response. Hannah explained.

"God's kingdom is something we anticipate with longing and great joy. We have faith that despite chaos, suffering, and spiritual warfare Jesus is a compassionate judge."

The three Norbertines, said they too welcomed Christ's Second Coming to initiate God's Kingdom on earth as it is in Heaven.

"Perhaps we are wrong," Abbot Joel began. "Perhaps the atheists are right. Perhaps God is a communal myth; a spiritual superhero who would distract us from the realities of poverty, famine, war, and death. And even if there is a God perhaps the Four Horsemen are the prelude to God's fearful Day of Judgement, but since we aren't able to know what Christ's second coming will bring we must act on faith informed by a compassionate reading of the gospel."

Then looking at his fellow Norbertines who nodded agreement Joel went on.

''We pray for God to forgive our enemies, including Hitler."

When Abbot Joel was finished the pope's trusted advisors settled into silent prayer for their fellow human beings. Present and past.

Printed in the United States
by Baker & Taylor Publisher Services